I0678423

Mimi

Trina Beasley

B. GLOBAL PUBLISHING

Mimi:

Trina Beasley

Mimi: The Lost Child
Copyright © 2015 Trina Beasley
B. Global Publishing
CML Collective, LLC

All Rights Reserved. No part of this publication may be reproduced in any form
or by any means without written permission by the author and publisher.

ISBN: 978-0-9965899-9-4

First Printing October 2015
Printed in the United States of America

For Jarvis

Thank You

Without these people this book would still be pages in my notebook
Riccardo Harris
Kevin Harrison
Christina Long

Contents

PART 1

1

Big Momma

Big Momma watched Latoya slip out of the back door, careful not to let the door slam behind her. The child was foolish to think that after all of the years running in and out the house, Big Momma would not notice her sneaking off again.

No amount of light stepping or catching the back door before it slammed shut would have kept Big Momma from knowing it was happening again. Another giveaway was the little black duffel bag hastily flung over Latoya's shoulder, bulging with garments haphazardly stuffed inside.

'Everybody loves love, but love don't love no damn body,' Big Momma thought while watching her only child switch rapidly down the street. Each determined step Latoya took was another step further from Big Momma and another prick to Big Momma's heart. The slow dawning of a sobering reality came over Big Momma. This time, the distance felt permanent.

She jerked her head away from the window. As she did, Big Momma's mind wandered back to the hell and high water her daughter put her through since birth.

'Must have been in the womb when the child made up her mind to do wrong. For one thing, the child was born breach — came out legs first, kicking, screaming and gargling blood,' Big Momma thought. *'Bout tore me to pieces. Doctor don't know how either one of us lived through the whole ordeal. Since that day, she ain't been nothing but trouble. The child is forever in some type of mess.'*

It did not get any easier once her daughter had entered school, either. The fighting with teachers, cussing out principals — and everything in between — was all angrily written out by frustrated educators on endless "incident reports."

But all that was child's play compared with this last move of hers.

Big Momma's grandmother always said, "Beware, 'cause when they

3

start smelling they own ass and realize it's for more than just pissing, the shit is bound to hit the fan. And when it does, the shit gets to everybody in caring distance."

Inside that "caring distance" was Mimi, Latoya's own flesh and blood; her baby girl.

"Mimi ain't gonna understand this one," Big Momma mumbled to herself looking back toward the direction her daughter was walking. Latoya's image was slowly fading away.

Big Momma knew that Mimi was planning on Latoya being in her life for good this time around. Latoya even told the child that the next time she left, Mimi could come, too.

Mimi had not been this upbeat in years. She even carried her momma's promise in a clear purse for the world to see. Mimi told her best friend, Stacy, and even told her teachers at school about going away with her momma soon.

"Soon" was the only timeframe Mimi was able to give them because it was all she knew.

Mimi used to fantasize about the trip, becoming a chatterbox full of hope and questions.

"Big Momma, when we leave, I promise I'll write you every night," Mimi would say. "Big Momma, will you teach me how to make dumplings from scratch 'cause Momma don't know how and I'm gonna need me some dumplings on Sundays after church."

Then turning to Latoya, Mimi would innocently ask, "Am I still gonna go to church?"

The child's pretty dark face would be so full of anticipation. It was a face that knew nothing of the lie her mother had handed her in the form of a dream.

"Yea baby, you can go wherever you wanna go, but if you get tired of church and all those funny-acting Christians, you don't have to keep going," Latoya would tell her daughter.

Big Momma would sit in her easy chair, wearing her favorite housedress, listening to Mimi make plans that would not make it past the front door. She knew all along that Latoya was not going to take Mimi anywhere.

A time or two, Big Momma started to state the obvious, but quickly changed her mind. She had done enough yelling and fussing at Latoya to last *two* lifetimes. Plus, age had made her bark less frightening. Once upon a time, she could read Latoya like the Holy Bible. She would tell her to stop lying to the damn girl; let Latoya know up-front she ain't never kept a promise in her life unless it was to a no-good nigga.

Nowadays, all Big Mama's complaining only made Mimi mad at her. Mimi worshipped her mother. Latoya was able to give Mimi something Big Momma could not provide: motherly love. The way Mimi looked into Latoya's eyes was a look that movies could not even recreate. The girl loved her mother, and felt like anything said against her mother was something said against her. Big Momma did not blame her granddaughter for that because that was the order of things and the way it should have been. The problem was that Latoya did not have the same unconditional love for Mimi.

Latoya's absolute love appeared to only be for men. Latoya's smooth ebony skin and deep gray eyes only seemed to hold men's attention for so long; long enough for them to live out a fantasy of being touched, pulled, and squeezed, and, after the job was done, Latoya was thrown to the streets. Her relationships were about as short as her attention span toward her daughter.

With this most recent departure, Big Momma decided to allow Mimi to baste in her mother's lies. She knew it would be months — maybe even years —before the child set eyes on her mother again.

Big Momma pulled away from the window with a new realization: things would be easier for the two of them with Latoya gone. Big Momma knew it would be up to her to pick up Mimi's shattered dreams and follow through on a few promises that could be kept.

At the end of the day, Mimi could shed tears in a big bowl of hot, steaming, homemade dumplings.

2

Stacy Williams

Stacy saw Mimi flash a note at her during Sunday School. She immediately grew nervous thinking Mimi would actually pass the note during class. Lately, these were not normal notes — the kind that told the latest gossip like who kissed who, or who slept with who. These notes were about Mimi and her own nightly escapades. They most certainly were not the type of notes that needed to be written in Sunday School or passed during services. The last thing Stacy needed was Mrs. Pines to catch them passing notes, read the notes and then inform their parents — well, her parents and Mimi's grandma because Latoya had recently run off again. She just up and left without telling Mimi, "Bye."

Stacy knew Latoya promised that Mimi could come with her this time.

'I'm kinda glad she left without Mimi because it's hard finding a best friend, especially a friend as crazy and fun as Mimi,' Stacy thought.

Other girls just could not compare to her best friend. Mimi did the wildest things without a second thought about the consequences. Stacy remembered back four years ago when they were in the seventh grade. During a water fight at school, Mimi took a trash can, filled it with water and poured it down the main hall.

It was the funniest thing ever to see all those students and teachers slipping, sliding and crashing into walls and each other.

That was Mimi, a real lover of excitement. She was good at stealing grade books and changing grades. She would take a chance on anything. The strangest thing was the fact that she never got caught. She had the luck of a leprechaun when it came to being

6

mischievous.

The thought of reading the note brought Stacy's thoughts back to the classroom and she raised her hand to get the teacher's attention.

Honestly, Stacy did not even want to read the note — at least not at church. Maybe if she stayed in the restroom long enough, Sunday School would be over and she and Mimi could sit next to each other during service so Mimi could just tell her what happened last night and they could bypass the risk of getting in trouble.

"Yes," Mrs. Pines said, finally answering Stacy's raised hand. "What do you need?"

"May I please go to the restroom?"

"Yes, but hurry back."

Stacy quickly rushed out of class, but not before Mimi pushed the note in her hand. Once in the restroom, Stacy was able to breathe a sigh of relief. She unfolded the note and began reading it.

Hey girl,

Why you so damn scared all the time? The look on your face was 'bout to give us away. Mrs. Pines ain't thinking about your scary ass. She too busy wondering where that sorry ass husband of hers was last night. Yep, you guessed it, over to Ms. Nancy's again but she knows all that.

Anyway, the reason for my writing is because I was with Big Boi last night and he had it going on! He copped weed, drank and everything! We partied ALL NIGHT LONG! Big Momma almost caught me coming in, but I dodged her slow fat ass. I don't know how I was able to get up and come to church, but I'm here. We did some freaky ass shit last night. That nigga is off the chain! You remember I told you about the black vibrating toy? Never mind. I gotta tell you that part in person. He even asked me to be his girl. I told him yea, but honestly, I don't know about all that.

I kinda got a thing for Tony. He's soft and all but he's different. Besides, Big Momma likes him. She loves a church boy and Tony plays that role good. If I do decide to have a main man, I think Tony will be him. He ain't like most of these niggas runnin' around here. Ass ain't his only agenda. He listens to me and refuses to let his life be the only thing we talk about. I get tired of listening to niggas brag on all they cash, cars, and anything else that makes them feel big. Tony kind of makes me feel like a lady (ha ha). Anyways, enough of that. I won't see you during services. I'm slippin' out.

Girls 4-Ever.

Stacy tore the note into small pieces and flushed it down the toilet.

'All Mrs. Pines needs to know is that we know Mr. Pines was over to Ms. Nancy's again, and trouble is going to pop off,' Stacy thought.

Mimi had been seeing Mr. Pines' car parked there since her late-night creeping with Big Boi started four months ago. She even caught a glimpse of the two of them doing it one night when they didn't close the curtains. Why Mr. Pines would step out on sweet Mrs. Pines for a lush like Ms. Nancy did not add up to Stacy, but she had always heard about men who loved whores. Guess that included drunken whores, too.

Stacy washed her hands and looked at herself in the mirror. She had a smooth, chestnut-brown complexion and shoulder-length sandy-red hair. Her eyes were a deep brown and a few dark brown freckles faintly dotted her cheeks. She did not think she was ugly, but she knew she was not glamorous as Mimi.

Mimi had a look that made everybody stop and stare. She was dark as her mother, with long wavy hair that hung down her back. Her big almond-shaped eyes were a deep emerald color decorated with thick eyelashes that had their own natural curl. Add to that a perfect set of white teeth, and luscious, pouty lips and it was easy to see how Mimi resembled a video vixen, and not the ones who danced in the background. Mimi would have been the one the artists were trying to get at.

Stacy did not understand why Mimi went around sleeping with everybody though. Boys used to approach Mimi with the thought of making her their girlfriend, but those were the boys she turned down. She seemed to only be attracted to the grimy, street hustling wanna-be dope dealer type, like Big Boi, Ray Ray and Man-Man. These were the type who lived in gambling houses, were always being shot at, or who were going in and out of jail.

They were not like Tony Knott, for example. Tony was street, but he was hella cool, not to mention fine. He stood 6' 3", was light-skinned and possessed a set of light-brown eyes that could command any girl in town to walk straight into his arms.

Tony hung out in the streets, but he hardly ever got into trouble with the law. He had a few run-ins, but nothing that landed him any jail time. He did not hang out with a bunch of hardheads and he actually went to school to do more than just pick up girls. In fact, Tony never approached Mimi in a disrespectful way. Often, Stacy would catch him staring at Mimi like he was hypnotized by her beauty but Mimi would not give him the time of day. Of course, she spoke to him and they spent some time to-gether as friends, but it was not the type of time Stacy thought Tony wanted to spend with her.

It seemed like Tony wanted Mimi to be his girl. Sex did not seem important to him. He wanted to get further than sex. No matter what rumors he heard about Mimi — and most were true —he still had her back. He even had a couple of fights over boys talking about Mimi in the locker room. His excuse was that they were friends and disrespecting her was disrespecting him.

Everybody knew the truth still no one dared to call him on it.

"That nigga is pussy-whipped and ain't even had the pussy," Big Boi used to say behind Tony's back. Stacy knew the truth, and the fact was that Tony did not stand a chance.

Stacy took one more look at herself in the mirror, shook her head at her appearance and headed back to Sunday School.

3

Mimi Walker

Mimi walked through the church hallway rolling her eyes at all the bogus women as they waved at her and pretended to be glad to see her.

'They know they can't stand the sight of my fine ass,' Mimi thought as she strutted past them.

Mimi knew they only pretended to like her because they knew her grandmother was crazy as Charles Manson when it came to her grandbaby. The fake respect they revealed was simply out of fear.

Whenever Big Momma was not around, they completely ignored her. A few even had the courage to say what they thought of her.

"Look at the bastard mixed nut wandering around," she remembered one saying as she walked past. "She probably looking for the father she never had a chance to meet."

Mimi never let them get her down. She kept her head steady, expression proud, and her strut in full stride, moving in slow motion letting her ample bottom switch fiercely from side to side for the haters' husbands to drool over.

Mimi was nothing like her mother, Latoya. The Latoya Mimi knew always appeared to be a people pleaser, permitting words and what people thought about her to control her life. Mimi felt that was part of the reason Latoya refused to stick around. She was forever running.

Mimi made up her mind years ago to stand up to the people she felt had pushed her mother away from her. This time around, it would be them doing the running.

Mimi wore her whore badge on her sleeve for the whole world to see. No matter what the women said about her, it did not stop their sons and husbands from lusting over her body with their eyes.

At sixteen, Mimi was built like a grown woman. Big Momma used to complain about the clothes Mimi wore to church but stopped after Mimi threatened to quit attending church altogether.

Mimi was shapely in all the right places. She had hips and legs for days, draped perfectly in tight, short dresses with hemlines that made knee-length dresses seem extra homely. The low-cut tops she wore always put her Double Ds on full display for wandering eyes. On mornings when she felt extra wicked, Mimi would wear plunging necklines to show even more of her cleavage. Mimi knew how to bat her big emerald-colored eyes in a way that would entice men and make them want her while their women stood helplessly at their sides.

So, most Sunday mornings, she pranced into service at least thirty minutes late paying all the women back for how they had treated her momma. Her fashionably late entrance ensured that she would get a captive audience as she switched from the back entrance of the church to the front pew of the sanctuary where Big Momma always sat.

At least once a month, Mimi wore a red dress that squeezed her mid-section and hips so tight that she had to put it on feet first and carefully wiggle it up all of her curves. Of course, she stepped into that particular dress after decorating her long, sexy legs with a pair of black fishnet pantyhose. She made sure her red stilettos emphasized every step she took upon the church's marble floor with an aggressive clicking sound that said, "Look at me, bitches. You may have run my momma off. But me, I intend to stay until I am ready to leave, so deal with what you have created."

All members of the congregation hated Red Dress Sundays. When Mimi entered the building, the air thickened with tension. Even the preacher's wife looked a little nervous as Mimi walked through with her head held too high and her top cut too low. The other women in the congregation sat in their seats with stiff smiles plastered on their faces, waving, but scooting closer to their husbands and boyfriends.

The men were in the devil's trance. Try as they might, most all watched Mimi's young, tender body. To them she was not simply walking to the front of the church. In their eyes, she was doing a striptease dance with her hips moving to the beat of inaudible drums. With each step, her hips bounced and breasts followed the same rhythmic flow. The men's eyes glowed as Mimi floated across the room smiling her devilish, sexy grin. The girl was a real piece of work and she knew it.

This particular Sunday, Mimi did not have time to tease the deacons and other male members in the house of the Lord. She skipped her sanctified sanctuary ho stroll altogether because she promised Larry, for the right price, she would give him the time of his life. That would give her enough time to chill with him before Big Momma returned home from church, which was usually around two o'clock in the afternoon.

A few minutes was all she needed to get this old trick off.

Mimi had recently started hustling. She had not told Stacy about her new enterprise, but she needed the money. She had plans for the future and being broke was not in them. Mimi told him up front she needed $150 for a head job and that was with a condom.

Sweets, an older prostitute who introduced her to the game, told her to never go down without a glove. Sweets was a renegade, a woman doing it all on her own.

Sweets had seen her old man shot down by the police years ago. She said she had been with him for ten years before the cops murdered him and could not see herself having another pimp take his place.

"These young pimps ain't nothing like they used to be. My man took care of me. These young boys don't know what the hell they doing and these young foolish girls don't even know they being mistreated," Sweets always said. "They treat you like shit and they like to beat the hell out of you for sport. The best thing to do is to stay down for yourself. You get in any trouble with the law, call me and I'll come see about you. But if I ever have to come get you, and Lord willing you won't be needing my services, it's gonna cost you a little something."

Mimi took Sweets' advice and decided to go at it alone. Larry — or whatever his name was — seemed harmless. She had seen him around town hawking her and knew he wanted what was under the tight pink shorts she wore the night Big Boi dropped her off. He approached her talking that nonsense of taking her "out to eat and shopping." She cut it all short by naming the price of what a date would cost him. Larry quickly agreed and all was settled. Approaching his SUV in the church parking lot, Mimi knew he would be easy. He seemed to be getting off just by gazing at her full lips.

4

Big Momma

Big Momma slid into her easy chair and took a deep breath. She was glad she had finally managed to slip from her Sunday's best into one of the housedresses she always wore. The tight girdle she had on earlier almost made her pass out during service. Had the Reverend preached any longer, the ushers would have had to carry her to the back and it would not have had anything to do with the Holy Ghost.

She used to always dress up before putting on a "few" pounds, which actually amounted to seventy-five. "Cute" was hard to find in her size anymore. Big Momma was decades away from the foxy lady she used to be in her younger days. Her once firm body was only a memory. Recently, she resembled a substance that lacked solid shape and she had the jiggles to go with it. In fact, it seemed more like she poured herself into clothes — mostly solid-colored housedresses because she refused to wear the ones with flower prints. Those made her feel like she was a walking garden.

The glowing cinnamon complexion she once sported was now a dull brown. One day she woke up and dark rings had positioned themselves permanently around her light-brown eyes that lost their sparkle with all of life's troubles. The long hair men used to dream of swimming in had mysteriously disappeared from her head. Now she wore wigs on Sundays and a headscarf the rest of the week.

It had been extremely hot that Sunday morning and cooking was out of the question. Big Momma had her selection of leftovers since Mimi was not around to eat with her. In fact, she wondered where Mimi had run off to since she wasn't in service that morning.

Deciding not to concern herself with that wayward child any longer, Big Momma settled on Saturday's leftovers, loaded her plate and sat down at the table helping herself to a pig ear sandwich drowning in hot sauce and a generous bowl of greens with plenty of fat back. Her entire meal was a health hazard especially since her blood pressure had been creeping up. She knew she needed to change her diet but, considering the circumstances, she needed the comfort that only a good meal could provide.

Big Momma's prediction came true about her daughter, Latoya. After Latoya broke her promise, Mimi seemed to shut down. Big Momma thought Mimi would bounce back after a week. But, this time, Latoya's lie caused Mimi to change completely.

This time, Mimi did not sit around the house, ignoring Stacy's calls, staring at her momma's pictures. Not this time. Except for the sickness and asking about her momma once, Mimi acted as if nothing happened. She kept on stepping; went right on with her life pretending that her momma had never promised her a thing.

Big Momma knew it was a front. The child did not know how to deal with her momma's lie. Mimi had adjusted to the fact that Latoya was not going to be around much but when she gave Mimi hope, it all but silently broke her. She actually believed her momma was taking her with her. Once Mimi realized Latoya had really left, "Where's Momma?" was her only question. Big Momma stood looking at her grandbaby standing there holding a packed pink suitcase, unable to speak.

"Gone," Big Momma said after staring at the heartbroken teenager. Big Momma knew sooner or later that Mimi would go off the deep end. A child just does not up and accept the hard fact that her momma does not want her anymore.

Maybe if Latoya had a drug problem or was lacking at home, her actions could be understood.

'I gave Latoya everything I could,' Big Momma thought.

In Big Momma's day, giving children time was not an option. Folks had to work to get what they needed and wanted. And a single mother working one job was not going to cut it. Working one job meant covering only food and lights for half of the month. Working two jobs meant keeping the lights on and groceries in the icebox all month long.

Take on top of that the no-good daddy of hers, Willie Joe Johnson, leaving Big Momma and having the nerve to claim he was not the father knowing good and well he saw the blood on the sheets after their encounter. He was Big Momma's first.

I didn't have much choice but to take on the responsibility of raising my baby on my own,' Big Momma thought stabbing her greens angrily with her fork.

She was doing well raising Latoya all by herself until another beau, Mr. Joe Parker, slimed his way into their lives. Joe Parker portrayed himself as an angel, but Big Momma soon realized he was the devil. He entered her life by way of the church. Big Momma met him at the grocery store but turned down his request to have dinner with him and told him they would have to get to know each other via the Lord. Joe fulfilled the request and took to meeting Big Momma on Sundays and Wednesdays during service. From there, they began to build what Big Momma thought was a relationship.

"*Tricked me good, too. Had me thinking it was me he was itching to get at,*" Big Momma thought.

That man dined and charmed his way into Big Momma's heart like a saint. It was not all his fault though. Deep down, Big Momma knew having Joe around made life a little easier. He gave her money and, for the first time in a long time, she had some real help. He had her thinking she could trust again— until Big Momma saw the tears in her baby's eyes and the bloodstains on her bed sheets early one Sunday morning.

I knew where he was. That's why I grabbed my pistol and marched right into that church house aiming for his head. I would have gotten him, too, if it hadn't been for Ms. Tucker's mute son standing in the way. Yeah, everybody in town knew I wasn't to be messed with after that. I dared the preacher to ask me to leave,' Big Momma recalled of the awful ordeal.

With a pistol in her hand and the devil controlling her emotions, Reverend Ranger decided they would talk about Big Momma's actions before making any quick decisions about removing her from the church roll.

Church ended before it started that Sunday morning. Big Momma could not remember how the gun was removed from her hand. She vaguely remembered Reverend Ranger walking her to the back of the church to talk things over.

After promising not to reveal to anyone what Big Momma had told him about the dog-ass man who took her daughter's womanhood, the Reverend decided maybe the old woman was not so crazy.

Joe Parker, on the other hand, left town.

'I think he knew I was a woman who was committed to finishing what I started,' Big Momma thought chewing slowly.

After that incident, church was a little strange or as Big Momma thought about it, a little crowded. People came from all over to get a glimpse of the woman who brought a pistol into the house of God.

She became an accidental celebrity. It was to the point that a lot of the women stopped talking to her. Maybe they were scared. Whatever the reason, their actions did not bother Big Momma much. She had never been big on friends. Latoya was all she ever truly cared about.

That was why Big Momma could not understand why Latoya treated her and her child as she did.

'I messed up a tidbit in my life, but I ain't never left Latoya out to dry. I always been by her side. Before Mimi, it was just her and me. After the Joe Parker incident, I even gave her a little more space than most girls her age. I didn't gripe about her hanging out with boys. I was just glad she was interested in them. I thought maybe after her experience with Joe, she might turn away from men all together. I knew I wouldn't be able to handle that ungodly situation. The boys she brought around seemed nice enough. I never thought any of them would do to her what her daddy did to me,' Big Momma thought.

Willie Johnson, Latoya's daddy, died. He never claimed Latoya a day in his no-good life. Big Momma could not even get benefits because of his uppity, high-yella wife. Yep, his wife was a piss-colored bitch, who had five children — all boys — by Willie Johnson. Neither of them had anything to do with Latoya, but that was just fine. God got him back. Big Momma heard one of his children was born with a condition. His oldest baby could not talk or something like that. Big Momma could not even bring herself to feel sorry for his child at the time. Of course, in time, her feelings softened — toward the child, that is.

When it came to Willie Johnson, Big Momma's thoughts were just as hard as her heart was toward that man.

'I would not give a flying fuck if he was burning in hell,' she thought, relaxing

in her chair with a now empty plate.

No matter how hard she tried to make things different for Latoya, problems seemed to follow. Big Momma even tried to make up for Latoya's shortcomings especially considering her own mother died giving birth. Big Momma knew her mother would have done the best possible by her had she lived.

Latoya was born in a storm of a mess and Big Momma knew she was to blame for some of her child's problems.

'I should have never trusted Willie Johnson enough to sleep with him. I should have made him marry me. And Joe Parker, that nasty-ass, sick baby molester, had no business in my bed.'

Looking back on the situation, Big Momma admitted she was lonely. She had been living her life so long for her child that she forgot about herself, leaving her feeling desperate for any attention.

'I will take the blame for part of Latoya's actions. Still, leaving your own flesh and blood don't add up in my book,' Big Momma thought. *'Lord knows I honestly tried to make things better for Latoya.'*

At sixteen, Latoya ended up having Mimi. The baby did not resemble any of the boys Latoya brought around the house. Mimi looked a lot like Latoya. She had the same dark complexion and funny-colored eyes as her momma. That silky black hair she had from birth put Big Momma's luscious locks to shame.

Big Momma was desperate to know who the father of Latoya's child was. Latoya would never answer when asked; she only stared at Big Momma. It got so bad that Big Momma started beating Latoya, desperate to erase the no-father tradition out of their family tree.

Big Momma told her it was okay if the father did not claim Mimi. They were living in different times than when Big Momma was coming up. Besides, the white man had ways of making lazy, sorry ass men pay for their responsibilities. It was called child support. Child support would have stopped that sorry-ass father of Latoya's from getting away without ever spending a penny on his child. Back in Big Momma's day, blood tests were not an option.

The beatings only pushed Latoya further away from Mimi and Big

Momma. After the first beating, Latoya left for a week. It was rumored that she ran off with the neighbor's husband, Mr. Stone. After he had his fun with her, he went back to his frantic wife and Latoya came home to Big Momma.

'I started to get my pistol and shoot that sorry-ass nigga dead, and then I thought about it. That man had a family and it wasn't no use in harming his children like my child and grandchild had been harmed. Taking a father away from a child is serious business. I ought to know.'

Besides, by then, Latoya was all grown up; well, grown in the body but didn't have a lick of common sense in the head.

Big Momma knew she could not start faulting other people for her child's mistakes. A few months passed before Big Momma took to questioning Latoya again about Mimi's daddy.

The second time, Big Momma got so mad at Latoya for not coming forth with the name that Big Momma beat her silly. Turns out, the beating still was not silly enough to force Latoya to make public the name of the child's daddy. After that beating, Latoya up and left for a year. By the time she came back, Mimi was calling Big Momma "Momma." It did not phase Latoya's dizzy ass one bit.

'It was me who trained the child to call me Big Momma and Latoya 'Momma.''

Finally, Latoya returned home and got settled in. Big Momma figured it would be best to let the subject rest and leave well enough alone. Besides, Mimi needed her momma, and running her off was not helping the situation any. Big Momma figured that it was no use in trying to get milk from a turnip. Strangest thing was, even after Big Momma left her alone about the baby's father, Latoya still took to leaving. She would come home in seasons. Springtime she showed up like flowers that blossomed every year. Fall meant a possibility, not a promise. During the summer and winter, she was a no-show.

Mimi never opened a single present with her momma on Christmas day. She was lucky if a card showed up acknowledging the fact that she had a mother who thought of her at all. When a card did arrive, Mimi treasured it like Santa himself sent it to her, never mind the fact that Big Momma had worked overtime for the ungrateful brat's $50 jeans she claimed she would die without.

Big Momma laughed aloud at her last thought.

'Yea, I used to be a bit jealous of the attention Mimi gave to Latoya. Wasn't I the one who spent all the time with her? For Mimi, I was able to do things I couldn't dare dream of doing with my mother.'

By the time Mimi came along, Big Momma had a little savings and had made supervisor at the hotel she was cleaning for umpteen years. She was even able to drop the extra job at the washhouse. Mimi participated in Brownie and Girl Scout troops and played in the school band. She played the trumpet pretty good. Big Momma even managed to become a member of the PTA.

'Ain't that some shit?' Big Momma thought with a chuckle. *'Never in a zillion years did I see myself in that position mingling with all those parents I could give two shits about, going out of my way to keep up with the younger married mothers. My grandbaby was just as good as they babies and Mimi was going to know that. She didn't need both parents to make her feel whole.'*

Mimi was blessed and cursed from the start with good looks, Big Momma soon learned. She walked around like a peacock with her head held high as anybody else's in her classroom. Buying her things to make Mimi feel better seemed to work at first. Then it happened; that damn mother-daughter poetry contest. It was Mimi's fifth grade year when things changed and Mimi realized she was different. Mimi wrote the prettiest poem Big Momma ever heard called, "My Momma is an Angel":

Momma has to be an angel 'cause they say the Lord is always felt but never seen.
I kinda feel like that's how my momma watches over me.

No, I don't see her on a daily. The situation with daddy is unknown. But, to be honest, that don't bother me none.

A momma I could get used to physically being around.
I'd love to greet her each morning,
promise I'd never wear a frown. Don't frown as much as I could keep a positive head on.

'Cause momma is an angel and, in spirit, she never leaves me alone.

The poem came in first place. Big Momma was so excited about going to the ceremony and Mimi receiving the award. She was not getting just any old certificate paper, either.

'My baby was getting a plaque!' Big Momma recalled.

The principal was holding a special dinner and the poem was put in some sort of book.

Big Momma went out and bought herself a new dress and a new wig to top it off. The season was fall, and there was a possibility that Latoya might show. She had even called and Mimi told her all about winning the contest. Big Momma was not even worried about Latoya not showing up. She just knew Latoya would make it to the ceremony.

Turns out, Latoya was, indeed, a no-show. Mimi decided Big Momma was not good enough to take to the event and all but told her to go to hell.

"Big Momma, you ain't a momma," Mimi told her. Mimi stood there in her new pink dress, sporting her first pair of heels looking as disappointed as Big Momma had ever seen. *"The contest is for mommas, not grandmas. Everybody else is going to have their momma there. I wrote this for her, not you. If she can't be there, then I won't be there."*

After considering her choice of words, Big Momma felt crushed and unappreciated. After everything Big Momma had done, every prayer and every sacrifice she made for the child, Mimi still felt like Big Momma was not good enough to raise her. With all the pent-up frustration Mimi's hurtful words caused, Big Momma chewed into Latoya the first chance she got, telling her daughter off something terrible when Mimi was not in hearing distance.

'I turned on my own flesh and blood like a rabid dog 'cause the last thing I needed was the backfire of my granddaughter's rejection especially with her laying around my house looking me in the face, eating my food, and causing my utility bills to increase for my efforts to go unappreciated.'

Fussing only made Latoya spend more time away. It was not until the first day of spring that Big Momma got over the anger, the day she put away her childish actions. It also happened to be the day Mimi turned sixteen. And Latoya still did not show up.

Latoya was supposed to be at the dinner table that day. Whenever

Latoya did show up to eat with them, Mimi would damn near be sitting in her lap while they ate dinner together. It did not matter that Mimi was damn near grown. They still squeezed into a single chair; both of them smiling like Cheshire cats looking into each other's eyes with nothing but true love.

That particular birthday, Mimi waited around the house for her momma to walk through the door. She did not even need a present. Latoya would have been the perfect gift. Time kept moving, but no Latoya. It was not until around midnight that Mimi gave up hope that her momma would walk through the door singing an off-key, "*Happy Birthday.*" Latoya's no-show all but killed the girl. Mimi fell ill and had to stay home from school for five days straight.

At first, Big Momma thought she was faking until she saw that Mimi was not eating any of her birthday cake or the dumplings Big Momma made for her. Big Momma could not even be mad at Latoya for not coming after the way Big Momma had been cussing her out lately.

Somehow, Big Momma managed the rage the few times Latoya did come through in seasons.

It was not until later in life that Big Momma realized how strong the strength of a daughter's love for her momma could be.

'Course I ain't never had no momma to compare such feelings against. So I can't truly blame myself; not completely at least.'

5

Sweets (Carry Witherspoon)

For Sweets, life was simple.

'Being a ho ain't as bad as people think it is. Yea, I sell pussy for a living. I been selling all my life. Pussy is the only thing that don't lose value when stocks fall. At fifty-three, I ain't half-bad at it.

'I must admit, time has changed things. Used to be, I could make a bundle in a week. Now, getting the rent and light bill money is a bit more challenging. The older I get, the tougher the hustle is. As long as these freaky, young ass dope dealers and turned-out tricks keep requesting my services, I'm game. I've even come to realize my looks ain't nowhere what they used to be. But the knowledge of my skills ain't a secret around these parts and practice makes perfect. I'm a mutherfucker when it comes to pleasing a man.'

A man has to be the freakiest thing God created, according to Sweets. She remembered having to pull her knife on one pervert because she wasn't into animals.

'I don't care how much money you offering. I guess he thought he was gonna make me have sex with his wife's cat. Hell to the nah!'

The shit Sweets thought back to doing made her feel sorry for the wives of America. Sweets looked nothing like the age that was on her driver's license. She might not have been able to pass for thirty, but when her makeup was right and her hair was done up, she could easily pass for forty-five. Even though she was up in age, she still had a head full of long thick hair. It seemed the older she got, the thicker it got. Her looks may have dulled through the years, but her shape did not fade. Her light-brown skin still had its glow thanks to all of the expensive lotions and creams she purchased through the years. Her butt may have lost a bit of its bounce, but she had a full rack that stayed perky.

She was not much on working out unless it was in the bed. As for her diet, she did try to watch what she ate because she knew from the start she never intended to have a job that entailed clocking in and out. Staying trim was part of her gig.

She also watched what she did with her mouth, too.

'I don't kiss none of my tricks in the mouth. I don't sell passion, I sell pussy.'

It was that simple. Everything about the job was simple to her even adjusting on a moment's notice to make sure her tricks were 100 percent pleased with her performance. She remembered, for example, having a trick request her services only to be pissed off when he arrived at her place because she did not look old enough.

"No problem Daddy," Sweets told him.

She knew his thing was making it with old ladies, like he had been fantasizing about fucking his grandma. Sweets went into her bedroom, put on a gray wig, a raggedy housecoat, walked back towards him with a slow limp, and it was on. Sweets knew that green backs ruled the world and people who believed differently were damn fools. Much as she could not stand tricks, Sweets dealt with them on account of the money.

'Don't get me wrong, I know love. I was in love with my first and only pimp, Dollar Bill. He taught me how to be true to the game. In the process, I fell in love with him. If he was around, I wouldn't be in this sorry-ass predicament, fucking with bad wigs and housecoats. He would be taking care of me. Yea, I know you laughing, but I know what I'm talking about. We would have a stable by now. Yes, I said 'we', 'cause what was his was mines and mines was his. That was how we ran things; as a team.

He took good care of me and, in return, I made sure his pockets stayed full.'

With Sweets on Dollar's team, recruiting was a sure thing. She pulled young girls in for him on the daily. If Sweets had to draft them in from the school bus stops, that was what she did. It was all about keeping Dollar above water because if he was living high, then Sweets was living high.

They had the type of arrangement going on that Sweets did not have to

stuff any of her cash to have extra spending money. Some nights Dollar would ask her how much she made and let her keep it all. He would even do that on nights when good money came in.

Even when Sweets handed him all the cash, Dollar was not stingy with it. Other girls they picked up would get mad when they saw Dollar doing it, but he did not give a damn. Sweets was his bottom bitch and they had to respect her position or leave because if he had to raise his pimp hand, Lord have mercy on the poor ho it landed on.

'Dollar never hit me. Don't get me wrong. Had I got out of line, he would have beat the dog shit out of my ass. I never gave him a reason to lay hands on me. The last thing in the world I wanted him to do was run into a bitch that was downer than me and who had more game than me. My whole existence revolved around making him believe that I was the ho game. Half the time he didn't need to make any requests. I knew what he wanted and made a move before it fell out of his mouth. I was always ready—anything from making bath water, to fixing something to eat, to bringing in two- to three thousand dollars.'

If Dollar was in a bind and needed some quick cash, Sweets made it so he would count on her. No matter what the situation, she was going to pull through. No matter how hard she worked the night before, she always saw to his needs.

'I worshiped that man. Dollar Bill was my religion,' Sweets thought.

Sweets had been in the game for more than half her life. She started in her early teens for money. Before men started paying her hard cash, she was always letting boys rub on her for candy, soda pop, toys or any pay out to cop a feel.

She was in sixth grade when she let Ray Smith, a tenth grader, stick his fingers between her legs for a red race car.

'I didn't have no more interest in a race car than he did. It all boiled down to him wanting to touch something wet and warm and me wanting a reason to be wet and warm. I guess some people are born for this way of life; others pretend not to be able to stomach it. Truth is, everybody likes to fuck, but some have to hide the fact that they like to do it.'

Sweets would come home with all kinds of new things. Her momma used to inquire where the stuff was coming from. After all of Sweets' lies about trading off stuff and selling candy, her momma did not bother to ask anymore.

'I guess she was too busy trying to keep my whoring-ass daddy home.'

Sweets' daddy was a motherfucker who married her momma only

because she was pregnant with Sweets.

When his parents found out about the pregnancy, they went straight to the courthouse. There were no church bells or wedding cake for them. They simply signed papers to make the relationship legal.

'Momma was happy as all get out but Daddy was only being dutiful. He was still a young man and marriage was not on his list of things to do —at least not at seventeen,' Sweets thought.

Sweets was pretty sure he liked her momma but was not sure if he loved her. Besides, her daddy had women all over town chasing him. He was a fine looking man who was thought to have a lot of Indian in his blood. He had a reddish-brown complexion, long, thick hair, stood almost seven-feet-tall and wore a million-dollar smile.

Growing up, Sweets recalled him being a wanted man around their parts. Some women would even flirt with him in front of her momma.

That was when the fighting would start.

Her momma and daddy would fight all day and night. While they were fighting, Sweets would be out trading and selling stuff.

One thing she did know was that her daddy loved her. He spoiled her rotten; giving her anything and everything. All she had to do was let her eyes linger on something in a store, and he would go buy it. Even though he worked as a factory man, he was such a hot commodity within the community that she had a suspicion that he got money for "personal services" also.

Sweets was his little angel, which was the nickname he gave her. If her daddy knew how devilish his angel was behind his back, he would have had a fit. Even she could not understand why she allowed all those snotty-nosed boys to fondle her.

'I didn't half want the bullshit they pulled out of their treasure chests to hand me.'

They would line up behind the vacant house a few blocks from the schoolhouse and give Sweets anything that was of value to them in order to do anything from rub her bare chest to examine between her legs.

'Maybe I just made them give me things to have a reason to let them do it. Who knows? Maybe I would have done it for free. No, I wouldn't. Not all of them.'

Maybe she would have let Ray Smith because Sweets knew he was good at doing what he did. The other boys made her feel like a science project, poking and pulling at her like mad men. Every now and again they might hit a spot that did a little something. Ray was older, though, and he knew how to make her enjoy his hands. He made her promise not to tell anybody about their encounters. Ray said if anybody else found out, he would not do it anymore.

Sweets never told a soul.

The sound of the phone ringing jerked her out of her daydreams. Nobody but tricks bothered ringing her line, but even they knew not to call on Sundays because she had the day off. Funny thing was that Dollar Bill did not believe in working on the Lord's Day. He was a good man, religious as he could be considering he was a pimp and all. Even though he passed, Sweets still kept the Sabbath as holy as she knew how.

"Damn! Who the hell is calling me?" she groaned thinking twice about answering since she was nice and comfortable laying up in her bed munching lazily on a dry salami sandwich and potato chips.

She went ahead and answered it preparing to turn down whatever proposition came across her phone line. Once, one of her regulars tried to pay her double to come through on a Sunday. Sweets lied and said she had the flu. She told him anything to tell him no without losing his business. It was not an easy rule to stick to nowadays with business being so tough, but it was a golden rule of hers. She did not have many rules so she tried to stick to the ones she did have.

"Hello," Sweets said with irritation in her voice.

"Sweets, I need you."

It was Mimi, the young tender who Sweets had just introduced to the game.

Before it was over, Sweets intended to have Mimi working solely for her. Time was flying and she did not want to be stuck sucking strange men's dicks at ninety. Her game plan was to introduce some of these young girls running around fucking for fast food and cheap knocks to the game.

Mimi was just the type of player Sweets needed on her team. She did not seem to be too attached to any of the young hotheaded niggas who followed her around, and she loved money—the perfect combination. Plus, Mimi was a knock-out when it came to looks. She had this exotic thing going on—real dark skin with pretty green eyes and long hair to match. Men loved that. All she needed was a stronger street game and it was on.

Concern replaced Sweets' irritation as she asked, "What's up? You need me to bail you out?"

"No, I'm not in jail. I just had a trick flip out on me!"

Sweets sat up alarmed, pushing her plate aside.

"Did he hurt you?" she asked.

"Not too bad. I got a few scratches on my neck and arm. I think I may have sprained my ankle jumping a fence to get away from him."

"Is he still around?"

"No, I lost him."

"Where are you?"

"On the corner of First and Main, at the convenience store."

"Be cool. I'm on my way."

6

Latoya (Walker) Wills

Latoya sat on the couch changing Little Man's diaper. She carefully wiped his bottom and gently sprinkled the browned flour on his rash. Anthony thought cooked flour was an old crazy remedy and refused to let Latoya use it on their son until he saw the cream from the pharmacy was not clearing up the rash. After one application of the browned flour, the rash all but disappeared.

Latoya attentively picked up Little Man and kissed him on the top of his head. He looked nothing like her daughter, Mimi. He was the spitting image of his father—dark with brown eyes. His hair was nappy from the day he entered the world and that was fine by Latoya. She did not know what she would have done if the baby came out looking like Mimi. It would have been too painful for her to bear.

She left that world two years ago and did not plan on returning.

Latoya needed something different— a pure life that did not include one-night stands with strange men that ended in disappearing fathers. Her momma had carried that legacy on over to her. Latoya figured she had to be the one to stop the cycle. So on her last visit home, she went intending to explain everything to Big Momma. Of all people, Big Momma had to understand where she was coming from since she faced the same unpleasant life Latoya was experiencing. Surely Big Momma would have up and left if given the chance to live a life without stares and whispers? And "living" was not working two jobs every day just to prove to the world that all was okay in her household.

'If Momma had of left me for better, I would understand in time. Besides, time heals all, don't it?' Latoya thought as she kissed Little Man again and began rocking him to sleep.

After sitting around the house watching Mimi worship the very ground her slimy feet stepped on, Latoya could not tell Big Momma the real reason she returned. Between Big Momma shooting evil glances at Latoya and Mimi soaking up her glory, Latoya lost her nerve.

She found herself lying and telling Mimi she was leaving with her. Why Big Momma did not tell Latoya to shut up and stop lying is something she would never understand. If she did, Latoya and Big Momma would have had an argument, which would have caused Latoya to leave the house and Mimi would have thought she would be returning when the flowers started to bloom, as she normally did.

This time around, she would not be returning for that sad celebration.

No, Big Momma continued to sit by and allow Latoya to sell her baby wolf tickets.

'Don't misunderstand me, I love Mimi. It's just that I love me more. I decided a long time ago I couldn't handle loving both of us, so I chose. There is no way I could have my new life being Mrs. Latoya Wills and give Mimi a decent life. It just wasn't working out that way for me. I would allow Momma to give Mimi her happiness. She had plenty of practice. She raised me. Maybe this time she can get it right."

Besides, Anthony, her husband, would have never proposed to Latoya if he knew she already had a baby. That was the one thing he disapproved of—single women with children. He always said that was what was wrong with the black race: black women and their lack of sexual control. Still, his beliefs did not stop them from having sex before being married. Anthony would always roll his eyes and looked disapprovingly when he saw a "welfare mother" pass by.

"They need to be more careful. Those women make our race look bad," he would say after the girl was out of hearing distance. "What could they possibly be thinking bringing children into the world without fathers?

"That's one of the reasons the government will forever be building prisons. The day black women start being more responsible is the day the whole prison system will shut down."

Latoya did not have the heart to speak up, did not have the guts to explain to him that she was one of those girls he turned up his nose at.

'I was too afraid of losing him.'

There were many times Latoya wanted to speak up and let him know the story behind the young mother holding the baby's hand. Instead, she stayed quiet and turned away, hoping that her eyes would not reveal her heart.

Anthony came from a proud stock. He was forty-seven but looked to be fifty-two. Anthony was short— nearly five inches shorter than Latoya— fat, and dark skinned. He was nowhere near handsome. He had tight eyes, a big nose, and a face full of acne. What made Latoya take to him was the fact that they went on six dates before he made any sexual advances towards her. She had never experienced that with a man. Anthony gave her the impression that he really liked her. Anthony made it clear that sex was not the only thing he wanted from her. He wanted to know her as a person. He wanted to know her thoughts, her dreams, her disappointments, and everything else that floated in her mind. All this was new but she liked it. She enjoyed being more than a sexual fantasy and found herself needing the positive change that Anthony had to offer. Latoya learned to ignore his lacking physical appearance and quickly fell in love with the abundance of love that he did offer.

Anthony's father was a preacher and his mother was a devoted housewife. He had one of those Huxtable families but without the girls. There were five other brothers and they all were married to respectable women. None of the women worked. They spent every second of their lives raising their children and tending to their husbands' needs or to church business, heading all of the women's committees.

Reverend Wills was a strong traditionalist. There was none of the new-style preaching happening from his pulpit. He had a large congregation with five hundred members. An outsider could easily consider it more as a cult than a church. Whatever the preacher — not the Bible— said was considered gospel. Any changes congregation members suggested had to run through Reverend Wills and his family for approval before it was even brought to the congregation for a vote.

Sister Hollow learned that lesson the hard way. She wanted to bring a Christian hip-hop group to the church to perform saying it was something that the children would enjoy. Her thought was that the music would be a way to connect to some of the younger street adolescents that the church may have been overlooking.

The idea never made it to a vote.

"The Bible didn't say nothing about no rapping," Reverend Wills said about the idea.

Sister Hollow was upset but what could she do about it? She thought about leaving the congregation but decided missing two months of services was enough of an act of protest.

The church had a leading role in the life of the Wills' family. Besides the church, children were also a centerpiece in the family. Between the five brothers, there were twenty-three grandchildren. Reverend Wills believed women were put on Earth for only one purpose—to have babies.

Anthony and Latoya only had one, Anthony, Jr. or "Little Man" as she fondly called him. She gently laid the smiling baby down in his bed.

From day one, happiness exuded from her child. He hardly ever cried and slept easily through the night. Latoya felt Little Man was her second chance; her personal gift from God. What surprised her was the fact that she took to being a housewife with no problems. What most women considered to be "second-class citizen status" suited Latoya just fine. She enjoyed the new identity that the Wills family provided her. It was as if they had their own perfect community.

None of the wives complained about the set-up. Everybody in the family got along. There was no talking about each other behind backs. All holidays were spent at Anthony's parents' house. In a houseful of crying grandbabies and loud-talking men folk, the women were to remain ladylike at all times. Only when Mrs. Wills' food was brought out did the womenfolk get loud. They all made a big deal over her good cooking. Latoya got pleasure from all the laughing and listening to stories about how mischievous the boys were while growing up.

'Wish those old crones back home could see me now. What would they say if they saw me with my father-in-law, the preacher, my well-kept husband and my non-bastard son? What could they say? They would all be jealous. All of them would have to swallow every word they ever said about me. They would have to erase all those thoughts they used to think about me. Wish they could lay eyes on me today.'

They had good reason to think badly of Latoya back then.

Her momma never had a houseful on holidays. She left Latoya at home to run amuck and make a mess out of herself. Most of the time, her momma was at work and would stumble in the day after Christmas smelling like must, sweat and bleach. There was no home-cooked holiday meal. Instead, her momma would heat up some bland plate from a stranger's house.

No wonder I found the time to get knocked up. Then she wants to blame me and accuse me of not knowing who the father of my own child is. I knew his damn name, but what good is me knowing and him denying going to do my baby? I refused to go about pushing a baby on a man. I hear tales that's what Momma did. She had everybody in town whispering about me and my no-good ass daddy. I never met the dog, and don't give two cents about his sorry ass. I just knew my baby wasn't going be chasing in behind rejection.'

Anthony eagerly accepted the lie she told him about her parents dying in a fire when she was twelve and not having any living relatives. Latoya told him she was raised in foster homes. She also told him both her parents were in their mid-forties when she was conceived. They were older when the fire happened, which explained why they could not make it out of the burning house.

All of the lies probably made Anthony have more pity on Latoya's lying soul; made him feel like he needed to be her sole protector since she never had anybody to look after her.

After telling him about her past, their relationship seemed to grow. He took to checking up on Latoya more. Whenever he saw her quietly crying, he immediately thought she was thinking of her parents. He had no idea she was battling her conscience, which would occasionally batter her with guilt for abandoning her daughter.

Anthony was gentle and extremely caring. He loved Latoya with his entire being. His love was nothing like any of the boys in her past that ran through her precious space and walked out of her life like she was a stranger, sometimes not even bothering to tell her bye.

Whenever Anthony held Latoya, she was able to pretend that perverted-ass Joe Parker did not exist. Anthony's voice blocked out all the whispers and stares women back home used to give her and her baby whenever they walked down the street.

In the end, Latoya calculated that in order to have someone so special in her life, she had to give up someone equally as important.

'Mimi would be better off without me, and Little Man would be better off with me,' she reasoned.

Alone, Latoya did not feel like she knew how to raise Mimi properly. Alone, she would not be able to raise Anthony Jr. She needed a husband. Did not the Bible say to do things decent and orderly?

'How can I teach Little Man how to be a man? A man needs to do that.'

Latoya's second-chance existed because Anthony existed. And no one could take that away from her.

7

Stacy Williams

Stacy could not believe what she was doing as she quietly climbed out of her window and crept across the backyard. Thinking her father could see her, she stopped at the fence and ducked under some bushes before continuing on her deranged escapade. Hiding in the bushes, the reality hit her of what she was doing. It was official. She had lost her damn mind.

'I don't know why I agreed to come with Mimi tonight.'

But Stacy did know. Her mother's golden bracelet, the one her grandmother gave her, was the reason. She had no choice. This was payback for being sneaky and taking that bracelet without permission in the first place.

'If only I hadn't took it out of jewelry chest, I wouldn't be in this predicament,' she thought.

Stacy had taken the bracelet to show off at school and ended up breaking the damn thing. The jeweler said it would cost two hundred dollars to fix. That was two hundred dollars she did not have and had no way of coming up with. She broke down and told Mimi about her dilemma. To Stacy's surprise, Mimi gladly volunteered to help her get the money. Once Stacy heard Mimi's grand proposal of letting her tag along on one of her infamous "dates," Stacy's excitement quickly disappeared.

"For real, Mimi," Stacy pouted.

"No funny business, I promise," Mimi assured her.

The deal was a trick got his rocks off by having someone watch him get down with a woman. Since his wife knew nothing of his fetish, and Sweets had a regular pop up on her at the last minute, Stacy was the only option. The trick paid both parties two hundred dollars for the performance.

Stacy reluctantly agreed. It was not necessarily that sex bothered Stacy. After all, she was not a virgin. She and Tony had been going at it for some time without Mimi's knowledge. It would not have mattered anyway. Mimi did not want him. But watching her best friend perform a sexual act was not something Stacy was into.

Crouching in her backyard, terrified of being discovered, Stacy almost reneged. Seeing what she thought was her momma's shadow in the window was motivation enough to turn back around, but Stacy calmed her nerves since both of her parents were heavy sleepers. Just as the thought, there was no one in the window. Her choice was made.

She took off, darting over the fence to enter a world she wanted no part of.

Stacy's heart was pounding as she rushed down the block to the place Mimi said would be their meet-up. With every step, she took a quick glance back toward her house. Though the block was familiar, it took on an eerie feeling at that late hour causing her to silently panic, searching desperately for her friend.

Stacy thought back to when Mimi first revealed she was ceremoniously a woman of the night. They were hanging out at the mini-mart with a group of friends from school when a strange man pulled up beside their car and called Mimi by name. She smiled at the guy and told her friends that she would be right back, then excitedly jumped in his car. Twenty minutes passed before she returned, patting the man's leg while he handed her some money.

Stacy was not even going to ask. She did not want to know. Mimi proudly volunteered the information. She told her she was no longer fucking for free —not even with her old boyfriends. Everything had a price and if they wanted it, they had to pay for it.

Stacy was speechless. She could not figure out what to say to her friend – someone she had known forever – only to find out that her friend was really a freaking stranger.

"Come on girl! Hurry up," said Mimi, who appeared out of nowhere. "I don't want him to find somebody else to do the job."

Stacy jumped back. She was surprised by Mimi's tone and her next-to-nothing outfit and arch-breaking stilettos.

"Girl, you scared me!"

Mimi waved her hand to dismiss her friend's worrisome ways. As she did so, she scanned Stacy head to toe.

"Didn't I tell you to wear something sexy?" Mimi scowled. "Damn. We can stop at the house and get you some shoes."

Stacy gasped, pointing down to Mimi's feet.

"I can't walk in those things!"

Mimi rolled her eyes and said matter-of-factly, "You don't have to walk in them. Just slip them on when we get to the door."

Stacy thought she had dressed the part.

She had on a tight mini-skirt and a T-shirt. Well, it was an old skirt she used to wear around, but that night, it appeared to be a mini. Usually, she did not wear skirts unless she was at church, and minis were out of the question.

"I thought you said I didn't have to do nothing," Stacy said stopping in her tracks.

"You don't and come on!" Mimi said dragging Stacy down the street. "Appearance is everything to most tricks. They are paying for an illusion. But I guess you'll have to do. Besides, he don't have no choice."

The tone of Mimi's voice almost made Stacy change her mind for the second time that night. They quickly back-tracked to Mimi's place, with Mimi barking all kinds of orders to Stacy. Finally, they were on their way to their destination. Mimi quit barking long enough to adjust her dress and freshen her makeup as they walked. Ten minutes later, they stood in front of the man's two-story home.

As they walked up the front stairs, Mimi took one last look at Stacy saying, "Remember, this is for your momma."

Stacy rolled her eyes but got herself together entering through the front door.

The lights were low as they entered the trick's home. Stacy closed the door gently behind them and exhaled nervously.

'Here goes nothing,' she thought as she turned slowly, throwing her shoulders back, sticking her chest out and stepping as best she could like

Mimi had showed her to give her body some extra bounce.

"Hey Daddy," Mimi cooed as she boldly walked in front of the trick who was sitting in a leather recliner. Mimi started bouncing and swaying her body in sexy motions as she planted her hands on the man's legs and leaned forward, putting all of her cleavage into his face.

Stacy stole a glance at the man as she positioned herself on the love-seat directly across from his recliner. He was not at all what she expected. He was a very handsome white man with chiseled features, a muscular frame and blonde, wavy hair. He did not look like the type to have to pay for sex. He looked like a family man.

"Running a bit late," he whispered letting his eyes run all over Mimi's chest.

Mimi started shimmying out of her dress. "Sorry about that, Daddy. Had to get good and ready for what I'm about to do to you tonight. Besides, I got something new for you, too." Her voice got really low and husky as she leaned in front of him now, totally nude. "I brought a friend."

Stacy dropped her head. Shame burned across her face.

"I'm breaking her in the game," Mimi said with her voice growing louder.

Stacy reluctantly looked up at the man who was now studying her. She could not tell from his expression whether or not he was turned on.

Stacy tried not to stare at her friend's nakedness as Mimi reached out to her and twirled her in what should have been a sexy spin, but was more like a series of stumbling steps.

Stacy's lack of coordination did not faze the trick.

A nasty smile slowly spread across his phase. He licked his lips and said, "Is that right. Well, come here then."

He reached out for Stacy, who shrunk back shooting a look of death at Mimi.

Mimi caught the trick's hand, and stuck the tip of his finger in her mouth.

"Hold on, Daddy," she purred. "She's playing the part of the Peeping Tom. When she is ready for some real action, you'll be the first to induct her into the hall of fame. Besides, you would not want to leave me all hot and bothered, now would you?"

Mimi bit the tip of his index finger and he squealed.

He must have seen the fear on Stacy's face because he motioned for her to sit back down. Then again, he was not worried about Stacy with Mimi on her knees in her birthday suit with three of his fingers, plus his thumb, in her mouth. Except for the shiny black stilettos, she was naked as a newborn.

"Besides," Mimi said tossing her hair, "How you gonna give my pleasure away? It's been, what, two months since our last visit? The wife needs to go away on business more often."

Then, they went at it.

He shoved Mimi on the floor and straddled her. They started getting down like wild animals.

Stacy turned her nose up, feeling so strange watching the act take place. She almost looked away until Mimi's lecture on the man's porch nearly slapped Stacy's face back into place: "Just sit there and don't look away," Mimi had told her. "If you're not watching the whole time, he'll dock your pay."

To make matters worse, the man kept looking Stacy dead in her eyes, getting off on the fact that she was there to watch.

The shame that burned her face now spread across her body. Stacy felt like she was invading Mimi's personal space.

'Yeah, we're best friends, but damn, I didn't think this was part of the contract,' Stacy thought.

The two bucked their way around in a circle to where the trick's back ended up being to Stacy. She watched his muscles bulge in and out of his back while he grunted like a wild beast. He worked his butt like a maniac, pounding to a fast rhythm that made Mimi knock her head against the floor. Mimi screamed for bloody mercy while he hammered her into the floor.

None of it looked enjoyable to Stacy. It seemed to her that if he did not stop soon, she would be a witness to a murder.

What turned her stomach the most was watching Mimi perform oral sex on him after he got finished humping the mess out of her.

Mimi swallowed his entire penis, and even managed to put his nuts in her mouth. While she gnawed and chewed at his private parts, he looked Stacy in the eyes, only stopping once he reached his climax. After the ordeal was over, he paid both of the girls two hundred dollars.

Walking home, the two did not say much. Mimi eventually told Stacy she could not walk her all the way home because she had another date, which was cool with Stacy.

Stacy managed to complete the obstacle course of getting back into the house without waking her parents. Lying in her bed that night, Stacy decided she would never take anything from her momma again without permission. She felt she had just watched the most disgusting act in the world. No, she knew she had just watched the most disgusting act in the world. She was not sure if it was the storyline of the whole ordeal or the fact that her best friend had the starring role.

8

Big Momma

Big Momma shook her head in disgust and disappointment as she dug around Mimi's room. Here lately, Mimi had all but moved out. The outfits that hung in her closet would put a ho to shame. They made the red dress she wore to church look like a wedding gown. These clothes were a million times worse than the trashy stuff she wore to church on Sunday mornings. And one needed to be an acrobat to balance themselves in those contraptions called heels lined up against her wall.

Mimi had turned into something Big Momma could not figure out, waltzing around the house and neighborhood like she was the cream of the town. The girl never did have good manners, but now her actions were unexplainable.

Mimi no longer crept in and out of the house. Nowadays, she came and went as she pleased. It was clear to Big Momma that school was not an option for the child. Big Momma realized that fussing about her doings only made Mimi imitate her momma, Latoya. Mimi would leave for weeks after each argument, making Big Momma regret she had ever opened her mouth about her actions.

When Mimi was gone, Big Momma was lonely. Mimi was all she had. She had high expectations for the child. That is why she put so much into her upbringing. Things were supposed to be different between Big Momma and Mimi; nothing like the relationship she and Latoya had. All the things Big Momma felt like she did wrong while raising Latoya were reminder notes for how to avoid the same problems with Mimi.

It seemed to Big Momma that the Lord had a different plan, though. No matter what Big Momma did, her past always caught up with her. All the fancy clothes, time spending, and churchgoing was not changing a damn thing. Mimi was still imitating her mother—still being wild and unruly.

'Will I forever be paying for sleeping with Willie Johnson, believing his promise that he would love me forever?'

Big Momma rested on Mimi's bed. It was a long time ago, but she could recall that night as clear as day: him leading her to his bedroom while his momma slept quietly two doors away. In her mind, Willie Johnson was the finest thing God himself created: a tall, jet-black, handsome man with soft blue eyes and a body solid and strong as the words he told her, words she believed, at the time, to be true. Willie Johnson had a serious face that could become soft, tender and gentle especially as he escorted her to his bed. That expression seduced her and so did the special charm he liked to display—the charm that broke her grandmother's heart and made a plum fool of her all in one.

In the beginning of their courting, Willie Johnson was honorable. He pretended to be respectful of the fact that her grandmother raised her to be a strong Christian, and made like it was important to him. Willie Johnson would not keep her out late. They spent a good deal of their time together sitting on the porch under the watchful eye of her grandmother. He even ate dinner with the family a few times.

But once her grandmother started trusting him a bit, he took it and ran with it. He told her that if she was willing to go a little further than a hug and a kiss good night, it would not change his feelings for her and that them getting naked together would only make their bond stronger.

Big Momma believed every lie that fell out of his mouth. She did not believe they could feel any closer than they already did, but if there was more pleasure to what she was feeling, she wanted to know what it felt like.

Just like that, she took a chance and threw all of what her grandmother had taught her out of the window.

Big Momma frowned thinking back to Willie Johnson. It brought back recollections she tried to erase, like shaming her own grandmother. That woman never got over her having a child out of wedlock. Willie Johnson not claiming the baby did not help matters any. A blind man could see that he was her child's father.

'Latoya didn't look nothing like my people,' Big Momma thought. *'She was black as tar and had funny-colored eyes. Still, Willie Johnson pretended he didn't believe it was his. What pained me the most was looking at my baby. She reminded me of what I used to love, what I still wanted at the time—Willie Johnson.'*

"How do I save this child?" Big Momma said looking toward the Lord. "I done did all I know how. I tried fussing, but she done just like her momma—up and walked away, simply left."

Big Momma started crying and pointing at the ceiling, "You! You know best that the last thing I want is her to get caught up with some no-good man. He ain't gonna do nothing but sell my baby a dream. I do believe she done already purchased some tickets. Why else would she drop out of school and take to running the streets?

"Lord, please send her momma home. She needs what I ain't never had—a real momma. I know better than to fault you for me not having one. I know better than to question your decisions, but what I don't know is how to stop my grandbaby from following in my footsteps.

"My situation was different. My momma died of natural causes. Dear Lord, I don't know how much longer I'm gonna be able to hold my tongue. I'm praying I don't say or do something to run her off for good. I don't want her to do like her momma and disappear. I know I ain't bound for this world much longer. My soul won't rest properly if my grandbaby is gone amuck."

9

Mimi Walker

Mimi knew Stacy thought differently about her since the night she took Stacy to work with her. Mimi stepped out of the shower at Sweets' house. She had just finished turning a trick not even five minutes ago. The trick had a scent that would have made a dead body smell like perfume but his pockets were fat and he was not afraid to splurge.

He was a filthy bastard who had hair everywhere except on his head and the worst breath in the world. He had the nerve to complain to Mimi about his wife not sleeping with him. What few teeth he did have were rotten. Mimi could not tell whether or not he even brushed the ones he had. It smelled liked his body had not seen any type of cleaning products in years.

Mimi was surprised that he still had a wife. If it were not for the money, he would not have the relations he had with Mimi. The money allowed Mimi to let nasty men invade her precious space, at least that is what she would tell herself.

Mimi sat down and started putting Shea butter on her legs. Thinking about Stacy, she could not help but get a little upset.

The bitch had the nerve to try and walk out on me at the last minute. I refused to let that shit go down. I had to damn near bulldoze her through the front door. It was bad enough she showed up wearing that five-year-old church skirt trying to trade it off as a mini. I took one look at her homely ass and wanted to send her square ass home, standing there in that bullshit. I had no choice but to take her with me,' Mimi thought, rubbing her hands even more vigorously across her legs. *'Good thing the trick was too horny to notice the difference between a real whore and an imposter.*

'Actually, I think the innocent appearance turned him on even more. Sweets al-

ways said every man's fantasy is to fuck a little girl. She said her ponytail wigs got the most action. So Stacy's lost schoolgirl look worked out in my favor, anyway. Not only did I need the easy money, but I do believe Stacy needed it more than me. I wasn't the one in a bind behind a cheap-ass family trinket.

'She sat there glaring at us in disgust, as if she had never seen a sexual action take place, as if she was still a virgin. Like I don't know she is fucking my old crush, Tony.'

The action was not that bad to Mimi, anyway.

'It's fat, but it's small as hell,' Mimi thought about the man's privates.

It was her task to act like he was putting it down. All she had to do was make him feel like a man. Maybe it pushed his ego to have a witness, because, Lord knew, the poor bastard was not working with a damn thing.

No matter how hard he pushed and worked the muscles in his back, the sorry son-of-a-bitch did not get nowhere. When his body was on top of Mimi, the peckerwood was not doing shit. Her moaning was simply part of the many illusions she was paid to perform.

Mimi chuckled a little when she thought back to Stacy's face as she sucked the trick's dick. Stacy almost ran out of the room. In fact, Mimi saw Stacy's eyes bulge out of her head.

'Please! I bet she's sucking Tony's dick free of charge.'

Stacy had the strangest look on her face when they walked home. She did not say much to Mimi, and Mimi did not like Stacy's judgmental silence. It was the first time Mimi felt out of place in Stacy's presence.

She was not used to having that new feeling around her friend. Stacy had been Mimi's dog for years; the only real friend Mimi ever had. With her momma being an outcast and all, it was not like many parents wanted Mimi around. Yea, she was a Brownie and a Girl Scout, but that did not change the fact that most parents mistreated Mimi behind Big Momma's back.

Stacy's parents did not exactly approve of her, either, but at least Mimi was allowed to come around. Since Mr. Williams drove a truck and worked out of town, she figured Stacy's mom did not view her as a threat. After awhile, seeing that Stacy and Mimi were inseparable, Mimi was permitted to go over to Stacy's house and spend nights.

Mrs. Williams was very nice to Mimi. She always treated Mimi and

Stacy the same, regardless of whether or not Big Momma was around. Mimi did notice that when Mr. Williams was around, her mother stayed clear of Mimi's house. Still, Mimi learned not to let little things like that bother her. Mrs. Williams could have been like the other women in town and treated Mimi's mom like an outcast. The strangest thing to Mimi was the fact that Big Momma apparently never noticed the treatment Latoya and Mimi received. She was so damn smart at times, but Big Momma could be blind as a bat.

Mimi thought about Stacy's change of expression as she forked over the cash. All that judgment rushed off her face replaced with relief. Still, the sting clung to Mimi as they went their separate ways that night.

'She ain't making it easy for me to quit feeling this way,' Mimi thought, especially since Mimi spent all that time explaining to Stacy, beforehand and on the way, what was going to take place. Stacy agreed to it all.

'I mean, if the bitch was that turned off, she should have refused the money.'

Mimi started to keep half of it.

'Hell, the way she treated me, Stacy didn't deserve the full two hundred'.

But, Mimi changed her mind at the last minute.

Even though Sweets took a small percentage of her earnings, the hundred would not have hurt Mimi's pockets too much. Besides, since Sweets picked her up the night the trick flipped out on her, the two had become close. Mimi could say they were even friends. Mimi had been shook up and scared to death, even though she pretended everything was all right over the phone.

Mimi let her mind wander back to that unfortunate series of events after the trick pulled his ride from the church parking lot to the back of a building about a mile away. In his ride, she was all ready to perform the act and he changed that quickly. He started slapping her around and calling Mimi a "gutless mutherfucker."

In between the slaps, he said something about hating whores, especially slick, black, money-hungry sluts.

Mimi's first instinct was to get with him. He would not have been the first nigga she got with. She had never been known to be a punk, but something in his eyes told her he had plans to really hurt her, maybe even kill her. Ignoring her first thought saved her life, because when she thought it could not get any worse, he pulled out a knife.

How she got away, she did not know. All Mimi knew was that, some kind of way, she escaped his ride and ran her ass off in that skimpy purple dress and those black six-inch heels toward the first group of people she saw. The people must have scared him off, because when she looked back and his SUV was nowhere in sight.

After Mimi got away, she was too scared to walk home so she went to the closest convenience store. She stood there with one shoe on, one shoe missing and thanked God she got away. She still needed somebody to come and pick her up, though.

Sweets was the first and only person who came to mind. Besides, Sweets had told her to call if Mimi ever needed to be bailed out. Mimi was not in jail, but she felt running for her life after being attacked was a good enough reason to give Sweets a call. It took Sweets a few minutes to pick up the phone, but she came like she said she would.

"Girl, you gotta be a little more on your game when you dealing with these sick-ass tricks," Sweets cautioned her. "Never let them take you too out of the way from the strip. Some of these nigga's only agenda is to kill a hoe like you and me. Blood is what gets they shit stiff. Believe me, I done had my share of crazy-ass tricks.

"We the easiest to kill and get away with. Most of us ain't got no family to look for us and the police don't give a damn about a whore missing. You think they gonna waste taxpayers money searching for who slit a ho's throat? Hell nah. The only time a cop gives a damn about you is if he's one of your customers.

"Tricks can be your friends or they can be your worst enemies. You gotta go with your gut feeling when you dealing with tricks," she told me on the way to her house.

"What's 'gut feeling'?"

"You didn't get a vibe when he approached you?"she asked.

"No," Mimi said staring at the new battle wounds on her arms.

"What?" Sweets said, taking her eyes off the road and looking at Mimi like she was some newly-discovered animal at the zoo. "Baby girl, you got a lot to learn. Tell you what," Sweet's position relaxed and her eyes were back on the road. She switched into her con role. The blonde wig and blue contacts against her reddish-brown complexion did nothing to hide her age. If anything, the mix-match coloring made her look older— an opinion Mimi knew to keep to herself.

"I got plenty of regulars, and I know a few safe tricks who don't deal with me anymore on account they looking for some young tender meat. Most of these men are married. They been buying pussy for years and their wives are clueless about their extra-curricular activities. I can turn you on, but it won't be free."

The look on Mimi's face must have told Sweets she was not with it.

'Wasn't she the one who schooled me on the game? Didn't she inform me that pimps weren't cool? Even she, herself, had given up on pimps after her boyfriend got killed. That's what it sounded like to me—her becoming my pimp. I have to look at the whole picture,' Mimi thought.

Even after her scary ordeal, Mimi was not ready to give up the life-style. She was accustomed to the easy money and she liked the thrill of the game. The nigga could have her killed her and that would have been it. Still, he had not scared Mimi away from the game.

'I could have played the bullshit role and told Sweets I was through. In all my confusion, I didn't have the energy to lie to Sweets or myself. I had turned more than a hundred tricks since I started. Walking away from all that money wasn't an option. I watched Big Momma work two jobs with overtime and her checks didn't touch nothing I made in a few days, never mind two weeks.'

"How much?" Mimi finally asked.

A slick grin spread across Sweets' aged face. "Forty percent."

"Thanks, but no thanks. That's too close to half."

Mimi might have been in need of her services, but she was no damn fool.

"Damn Sweets! You can't be coming at me like that. Why you trying to fuck me over? I'd be better off gettin' a real pimp. At least he could fuck me physically after taking my money. I'm willing to accept your help, but the price is too high. I could see giving you maybe twenty, twenty-five percent, but forty? I think I'll take my chances going at it alone."

"All right, Twenty-five percent." The sound of her voice told Mimi she was not happy about the decision she had made. "But you gonna have to work your ass off. I don't want you turning down none of my business. I can't stand no lazy whore. I won't be accepting no excuses. All that playing sick shit won't work with me. Being sick is the perfect working condition for our kind; we spend most all our time in bed anyway. And whatever you do, don't try that holding out shit on me. My tricks and me are close. I've known most of them for years."

Sweets was once again looking at Mimi and not the road, but this time she had a treacherous glare in her eyes. "Shit don't get past me. We can be partners and work this thing the right way and make a lot of money or we can be enemies and fall out. I may be older, but don't let it fool you, baby girl. I'm from the streets, so don't make my ugly side come out."

Mimi went ahead and let Sweets think she scared her. She let her ramble all the way to her house about what she had done in the past and was willing to do in the future if Mimi got out of line. The bottom line was the fact that Mimi needed Sweets and Sweets needed Mimi.

At that point, without each other, the two would not make it. Mimi being green in the game when it came to selling pussy and Sweets' age made her once strong game weak offered the perfect opportunity for a mutually-beneficial arrangement that addressed all of the weaknesses.

In time, all worked out well with Sweets and Mimi even though Mimi ended up doing way more work than Sweets did. Mimi knew it was on account of men requesting her more. Sweets was old and her services just were not called upon as much as Mimi's, though Sweets was still getting some action.

Like she said she would do, Sweets taught Mimi a lot like how to have a "gut feeling" although she rarely needed to be on her toes dealing with all of Sweets' old customers.

"Look in the trick's eyes," Sweets said. "Emotions can't be hid in the eyes. If his eyes are fishy, don't mess with it. I don't care how much money he offers."

Before her speech, Mimi had no idea about that sort of stuff. Her dumb ass was just prancing around the streets thinking her green eyes and wet pussy was all the job called for.

Sweets also turned her on to the fact that some men would pay for conversation from a pretty girl. That part of the game blew Mimi's mind. Even when she was dealing with high school boys, she had to put out for drugs, drinks, and food, except with Tony, and only because he was crazy about Mimi from the start.

But it was not any kind of talk tricks paid for. They needed somebody to listen to their problems with their wives and Mimi had to pretend she gave a flying fuck.

She could not say something dumb like, "Well, why you with her if she so much of a damn problem?"

She had to say things like, "Daddy, she'll come around once she realizes what a good man you are." Or, with the family men, "Daddy, who's your boy's football team playing this week?"

Family men needed somebody to pretend to be a friend. Inquiring about their kids was a big plus, when, in reality, Mimi did not give a damn about their sons or daughters.

All she wanted was money.

Mimi would never have learned these things if it were not for Sweets. She was so into not giving a damn about nobody but herself that being considerate to somebody else's feelings would have never crossed her mind. Being paid to listen to a bunch of bullshit was not even an option for Mimi; at least she did not know it was.

Through all of the time they spent together and all of their conversations, Sweets was becoming the momma Mimi never had. She was not old and outdated like Big Momma and she understood where Mimi was coming from. What Mimi liked most about her was the fact that she did not judge her momma.

Even though Mimi did not show it, Latoya stayed on her mind. She was upset with her for promising she would take Mimi with her and then up and left. What really hurt Mimi's feelings was the fact that she did not show up for her birthday.

'I guess that I had made up the idea that, even though she left without me, come spring, she would come and take me away.'

In learning to bounce back from the disappointment, Mimi learned to accept that her momma lied to her. Just like Big Momma always said, Latoya was, indeed, a big-ass liar.

Mimi wanted so much for her momma to prove Big Momma wrong. Even though Mimi never said anything to Big Momma, she hated her talking bad about Latoya.

'I love Big Momma and all, but I loved Momma more. Wasn't I supposed to? I had to learn to look at life for what it had to offer me. And from where I stood, it didn't offer me much. My momma had decided to live her own life, a life that didn't include me. So now I'm living mine.'

The reality of the situation hit Mimi when her momma did not come home on her sixteenth birthday. She knew it was over then because Latoya had never done that before. For most of her life, Mimi had grown accustomed to Latoya showing up at that time of year. She may not have shown up on Christmas or any other holiday, but Mimi learned to accept her birthday as a true celebration. Even if she did not get any presents, it did not bother her because her momma was home.

They would spend the night lying in the same bed.

'I loved everything about her—the small chip on her front tooth, the smell of the baby powder she sprinkled under her arms and in her panties, the way her nose sweated when she got excited. Everything.'

Laying there listening to her momma talk was better than Christmas. Latoya always walked into the room after taking a long bath, naked as a newborn baby. She would smile, sit next to Mimi on the bed, lotion her legs and ask her to lotion her back.

The joy that came from looking at her was unexplainable.

'It was like looking at myself with perfection.'

In her young mind, her momma was perfect.

Mimi used to treasure the moments they spent together. Lying in the bed looking in her momma's face was like looking in the mirror. She soaked in all of the adventures Latoya told her of the various nice men she had met and all the good jobs she had come across. She promised Mimi every year that when she got herself together, she was going to come get her and they would live in a big house with lots of pets. Mimi did not even like pets, but Mimi pretended to want a dog and a cat because it seemed like something her momma wanted to hear.

The only time she ever asked her momma about her daddy was when she was young— about seven or eight. Latoya and Mimi were lying in bed together. The soft smile turned into a hard frown. She became a new person, somebody Mimi had never seen before. She told Mimi not to worry about that sorry-ass nigga. Said he was a sorry-ass, good-for-nothing nigga that did not deserve Mimi's gracing. She told Mimi not to concern herself with the likes of a nigga like him, and not to waste feelings on him.

Just like that, Mimi pushed the thought of him out of her head. Sounds crazy, but that is how much she worshipped that woman. She believed everything Latoya said.

'Momma promised me she would find me a real daddy and apologized for giving me the one she gave me.'

And she never questioned her about him again.

See, daddies were not important in Mimi's household. Big Momma never mentioned hers and her momma never had one. It seemed to her that daddies just made babies and left mommas to raise them.

'I figured if Momma said I didn't need him, hell, I didn't. I was banking on the new one she said she would get for me.'

No matter what people said about her momma, Mimi was proud of her because Latoya was her momma. She did not win any awards nor have an important position in life, but Mimi felt like she was important when Latoya was around. She gave Mimi a feeling that nobody else could give her. And when she was missing in action, part of Mimi was lost. She used to wonder what was wrong with her that kept forcing Latoya to leave. Kids think like that sometimes. She figured if her momma kept running away, maybe it was something she was doing.

Stacy's momma never ran off for seasons at a time. After years of trying to figure it out, Mimi decided to leave it alone because if Latoya did not love her, she would have never returned in the first place and that is one thing she always did do—come home. It had to be the mean women in town that forced her to leave, Mimi rationalized.

But that rationale broke down when Latoya did not show up for

Mimi's sixteenth birthday.

'I didn't think I would make it. What saved me was Big Momma. Her moping around crying and praying over me actually brought me back to life. I couldn't bear causing her so much pain. I knew my sickness wasn't helping her high blood pressure. I didn't want be to be the cause of another grown person leaving for good. If Big Momma got sick and died, I would have nobody. I made myself stop thinking of what I was doing that kept Momma from staying around.'

It was not long before Mimi figured it was all right to mention her momma to Sweets. Besides, Latoya stayed in Mimi's thoughts.

She told Sweets her life story. She told her the whole truth— her never knowing her daddy and her momma leaving.

Sweets told her not to worry too much about it because some things in life "we just can't change."

"Ain't no use in crying over spilled milk. But yo' momma loves you. As long as you know that, you should be all right. Yo' momma sounds like the weak type. And you can't fault her for that. We can't help the way we are. People are just people. You must have taken after your daddy 'cause you strong-willed. You can thank the no-good nigga for that part of you, whoever his trifling ass is."

Mimi liked Sweets for giving her some reasoning for why Latoya was Latoya. Up until then, Mimi was completely lost on the subject.

Big Momma never touched the topic. She just stayed mad at Latoya. No, she did not fuss anymore, but just the mention of her name and Big Momma's lips would tighten up like she just licked a lemon.

Even though Mimi stayed at Sweets' most of the time, these days, she still could not bring herself to move completely out of Big Momma's house. Big Momma needed her.

Besides, Big Momma did not have anybody else.

PART 2

10

Donald Johnson

Donald Johnson sat in the front row of the church enjoying all that Reverend Wills had to say. He and his wife, Loretta, had just moved to town, and they were shopping around for a church to attend. The three other black men he worked with at the bottling factory had suggested he try Progressive Church of God in Christ where they also attended.

Donald was not much of a churchgoing man until he and Loretta were married. After the birth of the twins, a boy, Donald Jr. and a girl named Harmony, Donald had taken churchgoing more seriously.

His children had slowed him down a lot. Marriage made him step out on his wife less but the babies made him leave his extra girlfriends completely alone. Now, he occasionally visited prostitutes. They were less likely to get him in trouble. No emotional attachment: twenty- to thirty-minutes and the ordeal was over.

Besides, he really loved Loretta. In the past, he cheated because he could and she allowed it. She had put up with his cheating ways all throughout their high school days. Of course, they broke up a few times. "Needing space" was always his excuse but it was plain to see she was not going anywhere. Even when he supposedly got a girl pregnant in high school, Loretta stuck it out. She was totally committed to Donald.

It was not until Donald's senior year, and his mother moved out of town for what seemed like the hundredth time, that he realized Loretta was tired of playing the dunce. He assumed things would not change between the two of them as long as he continued to pay her the little attention he always had. Donald soon found out that the old Donald was not going to get it. He needed to step up his game. A long-distance relationship was not helping the union any. With him out of town, letters and phone calls were not doing the job of keeping them together.

Loretta started treating Donald like he used to treat her— not returning his phone calls and hardly ever writing him back. Whenever they did talk, her attention was not on the conversation. She seemed to just want to get off the phone and get to whoever was waiting for her companionship. Donald had to face the facts—she was interested in somebody else. But whenever he mentioned her cheating, like he used to do to her, she downplayed the topic, accusing him of being paranoid and told him to chill out. She was pretty good at blowing him off when it came to the subject of her seeing somebody else. He must have taught her well.

Loretta was a sweet girl. Donald soon realized she was the best thing that had come into his life. She was with him before he made the football team and before he was known as "the man" on campus. All the cheating and mistreating was starting to catch up with him. Reality check: it had already caught up with him. Loretta's many suitors were beginning to fill his sorry shoes with no problem.

It was not like getting a man was a problem for her. She was not an ugly girl. As a matter of a fact, she was gorgeous. She had a pecan complexion and soft, curly, jet black hair that she kept cut short making her flawless complexion stand out. She had big brown eyes with long lashes and high cheekbones that revealed the Native American blood in her veins. Loretta ran track so her figure was on point. With Donald out of the picture, now she would be someone else's trophy.

When Donald found out through the grapevine that Adam Stance, his lifetime rival, was giving her rides to and from work, he knew he had to take action. He kept what hold of Loretta he could and, later that year after graduation, went back home and asked for her hand in marriage. It was not easy getting her to come around.

Sitting on her porch, Donald did not know where to start with his proposal. He finally broke the silence by explaining the reason he was home. He wanted to take her back with him as his wife.

She told him she still loved him but was afraid of what he had to offer her. He had not shown her much attention before moving away and felt she needed space and time before accepting the responsibility of moving her away and taking care of her. There was that word again: "Space." It was the same word he used in the past to slip away from her and date half of the cheerleading team. She had managed to turn the word on him as if it was a poisonous snake leaping out of her mouth.

"Do you love him, Loretta?"

"What are you talking about?"

"Don't come at me like you don't know what I'm talking about. I know you are seeing Adam. To be honest, I don't blame you. I was an asshole before I moved away.

"I know I wasn't the best boyfriend in the world. I guess I didn't know what I had, or should I say, I forgot what I had. But if you really love him, I know I don't stand a chance and I'll leave. I'll go on back home. On the other hand, if you don't have the feelings for him that you used to have for me, then I know what y'all is sharing ain't shit."

"Regardless if I love him or not, Donald," Loretta yelled at the top of her lungs, "I'm not willing to accept what you left me with! Our relationship, *my relationship,* was based on memories. Looking back on us, I was thriving on what you used to do for me. The time we used to share together. What we used to have. I can't go back there. I won't go back there.

"I don't love him, and I don't love what you have turned into. You made me look like a fool! I was blind as a bat. Had me so confused, I defended yo' sorry ass."

Donald stood up to leave then stopped himself. "What do you mean? You don't love me?"

"Like I said, I love the old Donald, not the new Donald—the Donald who treated me like an ass the last year of our relationship. The Donald who may have had a baby on the way but it turned out it wasn't his. How could I continue to love the Donald who made it feel like spending time with me was a chore? I have learned to hate that Donald. That is the Donald who made me feel like I did something wrong." Loretta calmed down and lowered her voice. "Baby, I don't feel like I know you anymore. I simply came to the conclusion that I was fighting to get attention from a stranger."

For the first time in their relationship, Donald was at a loss for words.

Even when he had gotten caught messing up, he always had an excuse for his misdeeds. He could talk his way out of almost any sticky situation. He was proud of his quick wit.

Not that day. The moment he needed words the most, nothing came to mind. He wanted to tell Loretta he was sorry but felt she would take it as a con and simply reject him. Had not she just read him like a book?

He did not know how to handle that truth. Her rejecting his honest feelings was not something he could deal with. His honest feelings wanted to tell her that she was right and he was wrong, and, given a second chance, he would return to the man she fell in love with.

Instead, he just sat there silent, unable to express himself, yet unable to give up on what he had claimed as his on the ride down to get her.

"No, I don't love him." Loretta broke the ill silence.

A sigh of relief washed across Donald's face.

"I do enjoy his company, though. He's very nice to me. He has no problem spending time with me. So far, he has kept all his promises. Our relationship is kinda like *ours* used to be in the beginning. Adam," (just the mention of his name made Donald's face frown up), "has the same proposal you have. He wants to marry me, also."

"So, are you going to marry him?" Donald did not know he could sound so defeated.

"I didn't say that. I said I *didn't* love him. Why would I marry somebody I don't *love*? Did you hear anything I said to you Donald Johnson?" Loretta was getting frustrated and he could hear it in her voice.

"I sat here and explained to you who I used to love and all you want to know is if I'm going to marry him.

"What I'm telling you is that I love the old you, the boy who used to cater to my every need up until he became the *big man* in high school. What I'm trying to get through that hard head of yours," Loretta's ring finger was now poking Donald in the top of his head, "is the fact that if I do decide to let you have my hand in marriage, I will not sit around and let you treat me any kind of way. If things don't work out between us, don't expect me to sit around and cry about it.

"I've been on the other side of the tracks now and I know how to find me some comfort."

That conversation was fifteen years ago. And even though Donald promised, he had not completely changed his cheating ways. The twins, however, slowed down the cheating a little. They gave Donald's life new meaning. He had the best of both worlds—a handsome healthy baby boy and a beautiful baby girl.

The babies looked nothing alike. Donald Jr. was the spitting image of his mother—same pecan complexion, high cheekbones, and long lashes. Harmony, on the other hand, did not take after Donald or Loretta. She had a soft dark tone and funny-colored green eyes. She took on Donald's father's image, an honor nor Donald nor any of his siblings were blessed with.

They were all blessed with his mother's likeness probably because she prayed about it each time she found out she was with child. The last thing Betty Jean wanted was a black-skinned baby. True, she enjoyed Willie's companionship, but his love had to grow on her.

When they first met, the last thing she wanted was to carry his child. Betty allowed Willie to grace her presence because he tried so hard. He went out of his way to please her.

She made it no secret that she did not usually date dark men. Her momma had always warned her of the trouble they would cause. Betty grew up believing that the darker the tone, the more evil resided in the soul, not to mention, if things got out of hand, someone would be left with nothing but a little monkey to raise.

That was exactly what happened.

Betty was so charmed, she ended up with one in the oven. After becoming with child, her mother had to accept the black-as-soot father of her grandchild. It was bad enough her daughter was knocked up, but Lord forbid the black demon would not take her child's hand in marriage.

Betty spent nine months believing she was bearing the devil's baby coupled with her mother's evil eye reminding her of what she had done wrong. Daily she was reminded that she had tainted the family's bloodline.

"Must have been his blue eyes that pulled you in," her mother would spit at her. "You have forgotten the bad luck a black cat carries just 'cause its fur has a nice shine doesn't stop the evil with in."

Betty Jean Johnson, formerly Betty Jean Stout, was proud of her appearance. Her very light complexion and European features were things she thought gave her more respect when it came to the African-American race. Even though her hair was more of an African texture than she would have liked, a hot comb took care of that small problem. Being that she was so light, most people assumed her straightened hair was natural. Walking around with a tar baby at her side, labeled as her child, was something Betty was not looking forward to. When her first son came out with a golden complexion, she knew her prayers had been answered. It was soon learned that the child had a clubbed foot, but that was something Betty figured she could work out. In his mother's mind, a deformed foot on a light-skinned baby was a blessing.

"What do you think, babe?" Loretta whispered snatching Donald away from his past thoughts. Service was over and all the churchgoers were headed out the door to get to their long-awaited prepared meals.

"What's that?" Donald had no idea what Loretta was referring too.

"The preaching, the church, the people, you think this will be a good place to call home?"

"Seems good enough to me. I really enjoyed the sermon," Donald lied, only catching the first half due to being lost in his past recollections.

"Settled then. Let's go and introduce ourselves to Reverend Wills and let him know we will be making this our new church home."

"You go ahead. I'll meet you later. I need to go to the restroom."

Walking to the restroom, Donald noticed Latoya, an old flame of his. *'What a hell of a surprise,'* he thought.

He had not seen Latoya in many years, and to run into her in Tucker, Texas, a small town he and his wife just relocated to? What a coincidence.

Latoya still looked good but she had a new look to her, a cleaned-up look. She could have easily been mistaken for the preacher's wife with her neat, white church dress on and laced white gloves to match. Latoya wore her hair in an up-do, which added to the refined person she was passing herself off as. Her manner was even different. She walked around the church with her head held high and had a sureness about herself that she had never exposed before.

She made Donald feel uneasy. He headed into the restroom without speaking to her. Besides, they both shared a complicated past.

11

Stacy Williams

Stacy sat in the lunchroom eating her tuna fish sandwich and pretending to be studying her history book. She had been invited to eat with a group of girls, but lied and told them she needed to prepare herself for a test. Lately, Stacy's grades were not what they should have been. She was holding a C average, which she managed to hide from her parents by having a twenty-five dollar unpaid library fee. Without paying the fee, she was not allowed to receive her grade card. Since she had never had problems with her grades before, her parents not receiving her grade card was not a big issue. Mr. Williams thought highly of his daughter's grades and concluded she would be able to get into a good college.

Whenever he mentioned college, Stacy would engage in a conversation about where she intended to attend and what courses she would take in order to obtain a degree in teaching. Of course, a bachelor's was just the tip of the iceberg. She was most definitely going to get a master's in education. All these dreams used to be real before she fell in love. Now they did not belong to her; they were her father's dreams. Now, all she wanted was a two-year degree at a local college so she would not have to be so far away from Tony.

Tony was all she seemed to think about lately. He was her world. Stacy's whole way of thinking had changed since he started showing interest in her. Before, she would never have thought of disobeying her parents. Now, all she did was think of ways to get around what used to be normal to her.

Stacy knew she was not allowed to stay out late to spend time with Tony. She soon turned study time into "Tony time." Instead of going to the library, she went out with him. Stacy always told herself she would study when she got home. Instead, she went straight to the phone and called Tony up. And just like he said, he was at home waiting for her call. They would talk on the phone for hours, or at least until her father made her hang up.

Soon, having to hang up only made her become more creative. Stacy waited until her parents went to sleep and started climbing out of the window. That "adventure" with Mimi had taught her how easy it was to escape. Tony was forever trying to talk her out of leaving her house to come to his, but his pleading landed on deaf ears. No matter what he said, she always ended up tapping on his bedroom window, motioning for him to let her in. Tony had one side of the house to himself, so his parents were no problem. Over his house, Stacy was able to play house in peace. They laid up like grown folks, impersonating a married couple. She never got tired of hearing Tony profess his love for her while they were holding one another.

Even though things between the two were great, what bothered Stacy about Tony was the fact that, whenever he saw Mimi on the streets, his eyes stayed glued to her until she was out of sight. Stacy would damn near have to take Tony's head and turn it the other way. She could not understand why he was so taken by Mimi, especially since Mimi constantly made a fool of him, pretending to care about him only when she needed someone to listen to her problems. She made it no secret that she did not give a rat's ass about his feelings. Stacy wondered how Tony could overlook that fact that Mimi was now an actual prostitute, not just a tramp going around sleeping with niggas for fun.

Stacy never mentioned how she felt about his reaction to Mimi. No matter how upset she became by his actions, she could not bring herself to talk down about her best friend. Still, it burned a hole in her heart that he would take a chance at Mimi if ever he was given that chance. Stacy did not want to lose Tony to Mimi so her insecurities fueled her intense desire to please him even if it meant smothering him with her love. The last thing she needed was for him to bump into Mimi with a little change in his pockets, especially since now he could purchase what Mimi refused to give him for free.

Tony was not the only thing that had changed Stacy and Mimi's friendship. Mimi had all of a sudden changed. It was not an overnight change, but it happened gradually. It all started three years ago, the day after Mimi's sixteenth birthday, the first birthday Latoya did not come home. When Mimi finally got better, she came back to school, but she was different. She acted sort of the same, but this Mimi had different eyes. They were still big and green, but they carried a sadness that was not there before her birthday. And, all of a sudden, she became interested in boys. She had always been a tease, but now she was for real. Used to be she would let boys rub her legs, now she let them rub between her legs. Used to be she would let boys feel her breasts on top of her shirt. Now she raised her shirt and let them touch her bare breasts. From there, the problems grew.

Stacy did not know what to make of her friend. All she knew was that Mimi was hurting. Stacy tried talking to Mimi about Latoya. Stacy wanted to know why Latoya did not show. Mimi got real mean with her for the first time so Stacy decided to leave the subject alone.

'I know Mimi. I think I know her better than anybody living, even Big Momma. Because I am her friend, I'm allowed to see the person she really is. Most of time she pretends for people, but she don't have to pretend for me.'

12

Willie Joe Johnson

It's true what they say 'bout not resting in peace when you chose to live an ungodly life. Mines was a hot mess, as my mother would say, and I been paying for it for some time now. I been tossing and turning from the moment they put me in this damp, cold, dark ground. Crazy part is, I don't know if I'm in hell or on my way to heaven. What I do know is that I can't rightly cool down. My body stays at a warm temperature that keeps me uncomfortably heated. Being in this little cheap, tight, pine box that my uppity wife chose for me —Lords knows I left her enough money for an expensive coffin —I couldn't wiggle and shake the sweat off my head if the Lord permitted me movement.

Like I said earlier, I wasted my life on what I couldn't change. I made it my sole purpose to change people's perception of me.

See, I was a big black fella — black as a boot. But I wasn't like most real black men walking around. I didn't slouch and walk with my head down low on account of my color. I walked with a straight back and my head held high. See, I had something most yella fellas would kill for. I had big blue eyes. My good grade of hair wasn't nothing to brag about; a lot of dark men had good hair. But my white man's eyes wasn't something many colored folks had, especially not colored folks as dark as me.

Those eyes got me more than my share of women. I tell you the truth! I used those eyes to my advantage. I made a lie of that old saying, "The blacker the berry the sweeter the juice, but too much black and it ain't no use," 'cause all it took was one look into my sky-colored eyes and most all women, no matter their skin color, wanted some of this black, and I was obliged to give it to them. These eyes of mines even got me a few white women. But my sole mission was to grab me a high-yella gal and make her my wife. I figured that was my way of proving to the world that us men with all this pigmentation were just as good as those who didn't have but a few drops of coloring.

Well, I found me one all right. She was a looker—so light, she could pass. Not only was her skin transparent, she had the genuine features of a white woman. She had thin, naturally ruby-shaded lips and a sharp pointed nose. Whenever a chill set in the air, she was quick to turn red just like natural-born white woman. Her build even resembled a white woman's. She had no hips to speak of. This woman was a narrow, tiny ol' thang. Her mannerisms were even superior to that of a full-blooded black woman. The only thing that was missing was a head full of natural flowing hair. She had the nerve to try and make me believe that she didn't have to straighten her hair. I let her fool herself into believing she had tricked me. I know what good hair looked and felt like. I had a head full plastered around my black face. But I went on ahead and played the fool role just to make her feel better about the lie she was portraying.

Looking back on it, the only change that came about was in my head 'cause nothing else seemed to move any. Yea, she was soon my wife but it didn't make the world accept me. Us getting married only made her change. She became mean-spirited. Only thing I did was end up hurting my own feelings. Seems like after I forced her to marry me with the baby, at least that's what she took to saying, things got worse. Things that had not been a problem before were now major issues. Her biggest worry was what color the babies might turn out to be. Seemed a foolish concern to me. I was more concerned about the children's health. Now health seemed good worrying material to me when it came to a baby but not with my wife. Her main regard was whether or not her genes were strong enough to cover mines. Both her and her mother took to praying around the clock to save the child's skin. What a wasted prayer, I thought to my-self when they could have been praying for the child's soul.

Not only did I have her reminding me of my skin condition, now I had that evil mother of hers constantly telling me I was not good enough for her daughter, accusing me of voodoo and all other ungodly acts in order to get her daughter to consider looking at me. My only thought was that they seemed to be the ones practicing voodoo. What else would you call round-the-clock praying for a certain skin tone?

Her mother could not stand the sight of me. It was as if my blackness reminded her of a part of herself she did not want to consider. I was not even allowed to eat at my own dinner table when she came to visit. Rather than make a fuss of the whole situation, I took my meals on the back porch, when weather permitted, and in my room whenever a chill or rain sat in. And what did I do to fight back? I worked my ass off. I had no other way to prove myself. I gave that wife of mines the best of everything. She did not wear hand-sewn clothing; I made sure she got catalog-ordered dresses. We were the first folks around to have an indoor toilet. I gave that woman the best a man—dark or light—could give.

All I got out of the deal was five unwanted children—all boys. See, sometimes, more than often, when her momma was not around, when it was just me and my wife, she would look into my big sapphire eyes and become hypnotized. The old fire that we shared before other folks' stares and whispers interrupted us would start to burn and we were at it like wild rabbits. But each time she got pregnant, all the nonsense would start up again. Her momma would come down with her foul stares. It got to the point where I did not want to touch my wife after the fifth baby was born.

Like a fool, I took to proving myself the only way I knew how—working. Eventually, I worked myself into this cheap pine box. Died before my children got to know me. Of course, they were stair steps, coming right after the other. They only know me through a single picture, which was the same print that was put on my obituary. Not many pictures of me were kept around the house after my death. That sorry wife who I worked so hard to please, up and sold everything I bought her. To make matters worse, she moved around a lot, living high on the land off my earnings.

None of my children ever been to my gravesite. I don't blame 'em. She didn't teach 'em much. I blame myself for being such a damn fool 'cause I had me a woman who loved me a whole bunch. I'm pretty sure our child would have loved me too, but I don't have the power to fix what I did wrong yesterday.

13

Latoya (Walker) Wills

Latoya stood over the hot stove stirring her lemon pie filling. The trick to a tasty lemon pie filling was constant stirring. Mother Wills had taught her that. She had taught her a lot about cooking and life being that she thought Latoya's mother was never blessed with the opportunity to teach her to cook properly.

"No matter how tired your arm gets, you have to continue the circular motion in the sauce because if you get lazy and start moving your hand any kind of way, the mixture won't come out even. And if you turn the fire down low and walk away from the pot, the lemon will have a burnt flavor to it. Everybody knows scorched isn't a good taste for no lemon pie."

The most important lessons Mother Wills taught Latoya was how to be a true lady. There was the lesson about how to eat. Latoya had no idea people were not supposed to put their elbows on the dinner table while they ate. It took some getting used to, but she managed not to rest her thin elbows on the edge of the table while she ate dinner at her in-laws' house. She also learned not to blab out a thought while men folk were having a conversation. A lady was to remain a lady at all times. There were just certain things you were not permitted to do. Most of Mrs. Wills' new teachings were easily followed, but controlling her anger was quite a challenge.

After being raised in the streets of hard knocks, she once believed that wicked attitude was part of her DNA. She was not the loud type of black girl who was viewed daytime television. No, she was not the Jerry Springer-type chick, who made a plum fool out of herself. Latoya had a quiet sassiness. She knew how to tell people to go straight to hell without being loud about it.

There were many days when the women in town made her want to cuss and act a fool. But because Mimi was with her, a lot of the time she would just downplay the situation and ignore the rude comments that were made about her. The last thing she wanted was to get into a knock-down all-out fight in front of her baby. That would only give people more to talk about and, trust, they already had enough. So many days, she swallowed her pride, rolled her eyes and ignored all the bullshit that was said about her to her face in the presence of her baby girl.

All that Mother Wills had taught her had paid off recently, as a matter of fact, at church. Latoya was able to keep her cool when she saw Mr. Donald Johnson and that dizzy girlfriend-turned-wife of his judging by the ring on her finger. At first sight of him, she wanted to run over and grab him by his big back and throw him out of the building while informing everybody who was in hearing distance that they did not need that kind of trash corrupting the sanctified glory of their holy temple.

Losing control of herself in church was the last thing Latoya needed to have happen. What would Mother Wills think of such devilish conduct? Not only would it make her look unfavorable but it would also disgrace the family name. Given the chance to start all over and gain a new family name, Latoya decided against her first judgment. Still, it took all the energy in the world to stop herself from confronting Donald about how he used to treat her.

It burned Latoya up that he had the nerve to sit in the front row of her church acting as if he even knew anything about the Lord. Not just any church but *her* church—the church she had worked so hard to become an important member of. She watched him sitting in service with his head held high all dignified acting as if he had never taken advantage of an innocent person in his life. That is exactly what he and all the others did to her.

"I wasn't good enough to talk to at school," Latoya was now talking into the pot of deep lemon colored pie filling that she continued stirring in that all-too-familiar circular motion. Latoya was so overtaken by emotions that she did not notice the tears rolling down her face and into the pot.

70

'Wouldn't acknowledge my presence. It was only once we were away from school that anybody took a liking to me. Once I had made it home, the boys would line up for my attention. Had me so damn confused. They would even fight over my dumb ass. Made me think that's why the girls didn't like me. Only thing I couldn't figure out was, if they like me at home so much, then why didn't they talk to me at school?

'After awhile I figured any company was better than no company. Besides, Momma used to always say beggars can't be choosy. I was practically begging for somebody to talk to me. Outside of Momma and Mr. Joe Parker, I didn't have nobody. That's why it was so easy for Mr. Parker to trick me into letting him come to my bed. Him being so nice to me, I thought it was all I could do to pay him back for such good treatment. I didn't have a clue about how this thing called living worked. And it didn't help my situation any with Momma storming in that church house with a gun shooting like a mad woman. That only made people stay further away from me.'

The pie filling was past done, but being in a trance, Latoya did not notice it starting to scorch. *People treating a child like a disease ain't right. I had nothing to do with how I came into this world. People in small towns have small minds. They don't let you forget nothing and use every opportunity to remind you of your misfortunes. That's why it was so easy for me to be taken advantage of.*

'Oh, they changing slowly, 'cause Mimi got herself a good friend. It wasn't like that when I was growing up. My only friends were the likes of hot tail boys like Donald. I allowed them to crawl on top of me and have they way. All I got out of the deal was a baby, that at first, I had no idea who the daddy was. It took years for me to figure it out and giving Momma the list of names she demanded would have only made matters worse. Had I hollered off all those names, she would have gotten her gun and shot me.'

The sound of the front door opening and closing pulled Latoya back into the real world. Snapping back to reality made her realize she was in tears and that the pie filling was ruined.

"What's burning baby?" Anthony asked walking toward the kitchen.

Latoya hurried and wiped her face. "The pie filling. I had to change Little Man and put him back to sleep. I forgot to turn the fire down," she lied. "Don't worry. I still got time to make another batch."

"Don't worry about it. I won't die from not having lemon pie with my dinner."

"It won't take but a few minutes to throw it together. I already done made the crust."

"Where is Little Man?" Anthony asked pulling Latoya way from the hot stove and closer to his warm chubby body. Anthony kissed Latoya intimately and softly squeezed her behind. She could tell he had a hard day at work and needed something to take it off his mind.

"Anthony, in the middle of the day? I got too much to do to be thinking of messing around right now." Latoya professed not to be in the mood but, honestly, there was nothing more she wanted. This was something else she learned from Mother Wills—not to be so easily available when it came to men, even with her own husband.

"Sometimes a challenge, at the right time, will keep the relationship stronger," Mother Wills often stated.

'Sorry Mother, but not today,' Latoya thought. After going on such an emotional roller coaster ride, she wanted nothing more than to be held by the man who truly loved her.

"Where is Little Man?" Anthony asked again, ignoring Latoya's statement.

"Sleep."

"How long you think he gonna stay sleep?"

"Until he wakes up."

"Well, Ms. 'Until He Wakes Up'," Anthony was now carrying her to the bedroom, "I got something to show you."

Latoya laughed as he laid her across the bed. "I bet you do."

14

Sweets (Carry) Witherspoon

Sweets sat in the living room counting her earnings for the week — well, counting what Mimi had earned for her. Turning Mimi on to the game had been a sound investment, even though the little bitch refused the forty percent cut that Sweets had initially requested. The twenty-five was not as bad as Sweets thought it would be. Mimi brought in a pretty penny. She had to admit, the girl worked her ass off. She was down for almost anything but sleeping with women. No matter what she was offered, Mimi always turned those requests down. Even though Sweets wanted the money, she had to respect Mimi for that. Most of the girls in the game would suck a dog's dick if the price was right. So, with them, a pussy was not a problem.

Business was banging since she had Mimi on her team. No more running from the landlord. Even he was tired of swapping pussy for rent. Now that his wife was personally collecting the money, begging for more time was out of the question. Sweets did not have enough fingers to count how many times she had to use candles in place of lights. Yea, she still had a few good tricks who requested services, but managing money was not one of her best qualities. Sweets was used to getting what she wanted. If she wanted a new dress, she bought it. If she saw a cute wig, she grabbed it, and would always worry about the other things later. Life had gotten hard since she had to regulate things herself. Before, it was always Dollar Bill's job to make sure all was in order. Him spoiling her was part of the reason she was having trouble dealing lately.

Having money to help her out was only the fine-tuning part of the problem. Sweets needed a sound investment. She knew she was not getting any younger and a nine-to-five was out of the question. Besides, she had never worked a legitimate gig a day in her life. Like most people in her line of work, she did not even have a career in mind. The only thing she did know for sure was that she did not want to end up in a county senior home. Those old people were dumped there with the sole purpose of them waiting to meet their maker. Sweets was not looking to go out like that. If she had to go to a home, she wanted to go to a nice one.

Lately, she had been spending a lot of time on the outskirts of town. Outside of the city, there was a nice retirement home. It was a big red brick building with a manmade lake in the back. Off to the side was a lot of land where horses ran free. Sweets loved that home, but the annual price tag they were asking was a bit too much for her pockets.

Having a good ending was not going to be cheap. Sweets felt deep in her heart she belonged in that building. She would love to walk around with her head in the air pretending that she was one of the well-to-do. If possible, she would even turn a few private tricks while living there.

The other day, she pretended that she wanted to look around because her "mother" would soon be needing a place to retire to. The lady at the door, a slender blond, did not come across too friendly toward Sweets, but she showed her around anyway. The first thing she noticed was the fresh smell of flowers and pine, unlike the shit and piss odor that poured through the front door of the county home.

Not only did this new place smell clean, but the inside looked like a palace. Wide doors and spacious windows were everywhere. There was an indoor and outdoor pool, an area that was used as a beauty salon staffed with cosmetology students volunteering for credit hours. There was also a doctor onsite, as well as an activity director who had lots of entertainment options for residents including bingo, dances, and pool parties. Leaving the building, Sweets knew she had to figure out a way to become a resident once her street days were completely over.

"What's up?" Mimi said walking through the door.

"Not much. Just sitting here counting my change for the week."

"Oh, things going real cool lately. I don't know about kicking it with Old Man Halt no more. His old ass damn near croaked a few minutes ago."

"The old freak pays good so you might want to reconsider that, and besides, of all the ways to die, that seems one of the best. Think about it. If you could choose, would it be getting shot, stabbed or laying in a piece of precious ass?"

Both women busted out laughing.

"I guess you got a point."

"And if the old freak falls dead, make sure you clip him before you call the paramedics. He can't spend no money from his grave."

"Sweets, you sho' is cold," Mimi said. "You want me to steal a dead man's money?"

"I wouldn't ask you to do nothing I ain't never done. Don't go and turn Christian on me now, not when the money is flowing in. What you think? God gonna let you through the pearly whites 'cause you left a little change in an old man's pockets? Every time I think you got the game, you say or do something to remind me I'm still dealing with a beginner."

"Fuck you!" Mimi yelled from across the room. "I ain't no beginner."

"Hold on now! Don't be coming at me like that. I don't know what dick you sucked that went to your head and done drove you crazy."

"Well, maybe that's it. I done lost my mind behind a bad dick. But remember, I ain't sucked no dick that you haven't sucked. These all your old customers, so if I'm crazy then you crazy, too."

Sweets laughed aloud at Mimi's comeback. "A chip off the old block. If you ain't me back in the day, I don't know who you is. Now, don't come in here with yo' thongs all balled up in your ass tripping on me. I ain't doing nothing but trying to give you some game. If you don't want it, that's cool with me. You acting like I wanted you to take the money for me. Had you taken the shit, I wouldn't have known nothing about it. It wouldn't be mine."

Mimi sat quietly for a moment. She seemed to be at a loss of words. "Sorry. I didn't mean to trip. It's just that I ain't been scared of turning a trick since the time I had to call you to come get me. Having a dead man inside of me ain't exactly what I want to happen, not even for some extra cash."

"I understand baby girl. It scared the shit out of me the first time it happened. But after a while, you get used to it. I guess being on the streets for so long has hardened my heart. I can't *stand* tricks. The very sight of a man paying for pussy sickens my soul. It's because I know they think so lowly of me.

"Tricks are nice to you up until they are done with you. I have had white men tell me to get my funky black ass out after they laid on top of me. I have even had a black man spit in my face and refuse to pay me, complaining that my pussy wasn't worth his dick getting on hard. Yea, my man straightened it out after the fact, but that didn't change the fact of what happened to me. Tricks will mistreat you unless they know you ain't gonna take no shit. Feeling sorry for a trick, dead or alive, ain't in me. I hope you never get to where I am. It's bad feeling to live with hate."

"I didn't know," Mimi said, wishing she never said those mean words to her.

"It's cool, baby girl. I know you didn't mean any harm. I just want you to know where I'm coming from. I know you got a Christian background, with your grandma raising you in church and all. Me, the only time I go inside a church is to get somebody to pay my rent or light bill, and here lately, I ain't had to do that. Don't get me wrong. I know I need tricks, 'cause without them I wouldn't be able to make a living."

Sweets got quiet for a moment. Her eyes seemed to go off into a far place. "Mimi, if you ever find somebody who is willing to accept you for who you are with all your faults, keep that person in your life."

15

Mimi Walker

Mimi looked in his fine face and smiled warmly.

"You one of the first men I done slept with for free in a long time."

"Well, I offered you money," Tony said in a hushed tone.

"I know. I guess I just didn't feel like working tonight. I wanted to be with someone for pleasure, not dollars."

"There a difference?" Tony asked with a puzzled look on his face. The room was dark and Mimi could only make out his facial expression because the full moon gave a bit of light.

"Yes, I don't think of sleeping with you as a job. Tricks aren't pleasure lovers, they are money lovers. Don't get me wrong. Some of them know how to put it down, but it's different."

"Different how?"

"I don't know. I guess it's different because I *want* to be here."

"I don't get you, Mimi. I mean, I spent most of my high school days trying to holla at you and you never gave me the time of day. Now that me and yo' home girl are an item, you give me a chance."

"I couldn't get with you back then," Mimi said. "You liked me too much."

She turned and faced him. They were so close that their noses almost touched.

"Tony, it may sound strange, but I didn't want to hurt you. You didn't deserve someone like me in your life. Now, Stacy? She's different. She'll love you the way you deserve to be loved. You are simply too good for me."

"Maybe I should have been the one to make that decision."

"True, but as things are, I was the one to make it. It worked out better this way anyways 'cause now you got Stacy and she's a sweet girl. Had you and I hooked up, you two would have never been able to become an item, as you say."

"She's all right," Tony said unconvincingly.

"Sounds like trouble in paradise."

"Nothing like that. It's just that she is smothering me. Like, I'd be willing to bet that, at this very moment, she is searching for me like Obama was looking for Bin Laden."

Mimi couldn't help but laugh. "It can't be that bad. And even if it is, it's only 'cause she loves you. I couldn't see myself loving nobody like that. Not without money being the reason."

"Why?"

"That's the part even I don't understand. Take you, for instance. I have always known what type of person you are all my life. You were never like any of the other boys at school. You liked me for real but still I passed you up. I can talk to you about *anything* and you listen. You don't just play the role for a piece of ass.

"Maybe the problem is, I don't believe I deserve something so pure in my life."

"That's crazy. You shouldn't think like that. You deserve just as much as the next person."

"Maybe so," Mimi said getting out of bed, putting on her clothes. "It seems I'm cut from a different piece of cloth than the rest."

"You leaving already?" Tony almost yelled.

"Yep, Momma got things to do. I can't be lying around for free."

"Well, what you charge? I mean, how much would I have to spend to see you again?"

"Sorry, but I'm not for sale to you. Don't misunderstand me. You are my best friend's man."

"That's bullshit!" Tony yelled as Mimi slammed the door.

Mimi strolled down her grandmother's street with her head held high, watching all the neighbors look at her in repugnance. Her tight leather pants hugged her full hips and her half shirt, which was at least two sizes too small, revealed the fullness of her DDs. A mane of long black hair hung down the mid-section of her back. She was a whore and figured why not play the role to the fullest.

Her profession was no longer a secret. Big Momma pretended not to know where all the extra money was coming from. Her only complaint was that none of the men Mimi slept with were decent enough to come over and meet her. Big Momma was still under the impression that she was sleeping around for pleasure. Mimi figured it was her way of dealing with it.

After dropping out of school, Big Momma all but gave up on the child. It was more than evident that she had her own agenda and school was not a part of it. Tony was not supposed to be on her agenda either, but something just up and happened. Besides, with Stacy treating her so badly, he was the only way Mimi could see to pay her back.

"All because I had her go with me to turn a trick. I paid her good money to watch me fuck," Mimi said to herself, still not able to shake the disrespect.

She walked through Big Momma's front door and headed to the kitchen.

"Hey, Big Momma," she greeted.

"Hey baby. What brings you around here?" Big Momma said dryly.

"Big Momma, please don't start with me. I came because I wanted to see you. I was hoping you had a pot of dumplings on." Mimi took a seat at the kitchen table.

"Well, I don't."

Lately, Big Momma had been edgy whenever she came around. She had started treating Mimi like she treated her momma.

"They don't feed you when they done having their way with you?"

"Who don't feed me?"

"Those damn hoodlums you running around here with."

"Big Momma, ain't that how you ran my momma off." Mimi stopped talking and wished she could take the words back.

Big Momma slapped Mimi across the face. "Don't you walk into my house telling me what I didn't do for your momma. I did everything possible for that child. Ungrateful! That's what's wrong with the both of you.

You think this world owes you something. Well, I got news for yo' hot ass. This world ain't gonna give you shit. Anything you want, you gonna have to work for it. And laying up with any and everybody's husband don't count as work!"

Mimi jumped up and ran toward the back door. Big Momma stepped in front of her to block her passage.

"Look, Mimi. I can't do it again. I can't let you break my heart, something that yo' momma had no problem doing."

Mimi looked up at Big Momma with tears rolling down her eyes. "Leave my momma out of this."

"Child, I don't have the energy to keep running behind you. Mimi, I'm tired. I'm old and damn tired. Don't you understand? You and yo' momma are going to be the death of me. I done spent my whole life trying to give you what I didn't have.

"You just like her. You don't see nothing unless it's pleasing you. I know yo' momma up and leaving messed things up for you but I could only do so much. Least you had a momma. I never had the opportunity to get to know mines.

"I love you to death, but I can't keep chasing after you. Don't you know I worry about you? Every time I hear a siren or see something on the news about an unidentified body, you the first person to pop in my mind. You leave here and don't come back for weeks at a time. Nowadays, even Stacy don't know where you at."

Big Momma grabbed Mimi's shoulders and started wailing, "And why you taking up with the like of Sweets? Why you over there living with her? Lay in the bed with dogs and you get up with fleas. That's exactly what's gonna happen to you. I been praying you don't end up selling yo' tail just like she is over there doing. And, at her age, Lord it don't make sense."

"Too late," Mimi said rubbing the area where Big Momma slapped her.

"What?" Big Momma gasped dropping her arms from Mimi's shoulders.

"You heard me right. I said too fucking late. What? You think I'm gonna take up your profession and clean houses for a living or maybe you had me picked to work at a burger joint."

"Lord!" Big Momma bellowed.

Mimi pushed her to the side and walked out the door.

Bitch. How she gonna put her hands on me? I ain't a child no more. I ain't never going back over there. I'm tired of her judging my momma. She the one who raised us, so maybe it's something wrong with her. I see why Momma left. I get so tired of hearing all that bullshit about what she did for my momma and me.

'She is the momma so she was supposed to raise her child. She ain't did nothing no other parent would do. All that griping is enough to drive a sane person mad. Well, she ain't gotta worry about me no more.'

Mimi walked down the street talking to herself. Her conversation looked as if she was complaining to a friend.

"And how she gonna talk against Sweets? Sweets is a good person. She make her living one way, Big Momma makes hers another. Hell, given the chance, I'd choose Sweets' profession any day. Fuck cleaning in behind a bitch that don't give a damn about me. Fuck cleaning in behind anybody.

"At least Sweets listens to me. She don't just bark orders at me. She is the only grown person I know who ain't crazy in the head. She may be a whore, but she ain't let the world drive her crazy. She don't complain all the time about how her life ended up. Hell, her old man got knocked off by the police. She should be mad as hell! The same people that are paid to protect her killed her man. Now, Sweets, she got a reason to be mad as hell, but she ain't. She just taking life with a grain of salt. You gonna have to swallow the shit anyway.

"Big Momma, on the other hand, she stays pissed off. Mad at Momma for leaving me, mad at me for living my life. I refuse to be trapped in this world waking up pissed every day. While I'm living, I'm gonna make me some money and spend it the way I choose. And I'm gonna make my money the way I choose. That old woman makes about as much sense as two punks standing at the church altar.

"*She's tired.* Hell, I'm tired of her being tired, 'cause all her tiredness been landing on my back. I'm tired of carrying her big ass."

Before she knew it, Mimi was standing at Sweets' front door. Mimi walked into the house and straight to the wall mirror Sweets had hanging up.

"What happened to you? One of them tricks go bad on you again?"

"Nah, Big Momma blacked out on me."

"What happened? You ain't over there disrespecting yo' grandmother are you? She got you pretty good. Looks like yo' eye is gonna be black."

"*Damn.* I was hoping that wouldn't happen." Mimi walked to the back room and laid across the bed.

"Well, you gonna tell me what happened or what?" Sweets asked following behind her.

"I don't feel like talking right now. I just wanna sleep for a while."

"All right, we can talk later. I had a few tricks for you, but I'll tell 'em something came up."

Mimi closed her eyes and fell fast asleep.

PART 3

16

Stacy Williams

Stacy couldn't believe her eyes.

"Do you love her?" Stacy screamed as she ran into the room to see Tony laid up with Mimi. Stacy stood on one side of Tony's room as he bolted to the other. Mimi lay in the bed with the covers clumsily wrapped around her.

Tony was grateful that his parents were not home because this fight seemed as though it was going to get ugly.

"Don't lie to me Tony! Tell me right now, 'cause if you love her then..."

Stacy rushed toward Tony screaming like a mad woman. Her dark brown eyes were narrow. Foam clung to the corners of her mouth. She swung her fists wildly at his face trying to punch him.

Tony grabbed Stacy's hand in mid-air.

"Then what?" he asked, holding Stacy at bay. "If I love her then what the hell are you going to do? Beat the shit out of me? Calm down girl! You don't need to be acting like this."

He had intended to stay even-tempered, but Stacy's unruly behavior made him lose control.

"You can't love her and love me." Stacy changed the subject, not knowing how to react to the boldness in Tony's response to her demanding question.

If he did love her, what would she do besides accept the truth that he loved Mimi? What other options could she create? Was there any other feeling in the world that could replace the feeling that overcame her sense of self when Tony was near?

"No!" Stacy screamed like a lunatic, "I don't want to play games with you!"

All she knew, at that particular moment, was that she refused to accept the fact that Tony did not love her. Yea, he used to love Mimi, but that was before he started seeing her.

"You told me you loved me," said Stacy, who was talking more to herself than to Tony, trying to make herself believe the words that came out of his mouth not too long ago. "You made me believe you loved me."

Stacy settled down. She knew if she gave him the opportunity, he would clear everything up. She was no longer trying to abuse Tony. She needed him to tell her he loved her and for him to make her feel like he meant it.

'Why won't he say it?' Stacy thought.

Was it not just that morning that he spoke those three precious words while making love before she left his bedroom? She could hear him murmur quietly the words in her ear all while he entered her warm spot, his spot. He had gently repeated those three words to her earlier so why not repeat them when she asked him the question concerning his love for her? Why Tony refused to reveal what was not long ago said in his heart confused her.

Stacy stood there in the longest silence, waiting. The seconds seemed to be laughing at her and the smirk on Mimi's face made her heart rate increase. Tony never said a single word; he just stared at her with a confused look on his face. She would know if he was lying. Tony was never a good liar. Whenever he said something that was not true, his lips would curl around the edges and lines would appear on his forehead. But, at that moment, he refused to answer her question. His only reply was him questioning what she was doing in his bedroom.

"Tony, please!" Stacy broke down in tears. "Please don't do this to us. I had plans. *We* had plans. Why are you letting her ruin our plans? She can't be with you. You can't possibly be that damn stupid. She belongs to everybody. Haven't you figured that out yet?"

While speaking, Stacy wore a mask of need and humiliation. She just did not get it. What was it about Mimi that he could not let go of?

"She is the one who broke your heart. This is the same bitch who listened to your dreams and then walked away. You know she doesn't care about you. She has never tried to hide the fact that she doesn't want you."

Stacy thought that maybe if she reminded Tony of all the heartache that Mimi caused him in the past, he could walk away from her. Maybe if she reminded him of how Mimi walked all over his heart, he would put Mimi out of his bed and tell Stacy how much he loved her.

Nothing. Instead, Tony continued to ask Stacy to leave.

"Mimi," Stacy turned to Mimi with a tear-stained face, revealing all the pain in the world. "You know I love him. Tell him you don't need him. Please tell him the truth.

"Look, you say you are my friend. Then be it and tell him the truth. Tell him to stop coming around. Treat him like you treated him back when he was begging for your attention. Mimi, why are you doing this to me? Why are you doing this to him? I thought you were my friend. I thought you were my best friend."

The smirk left Mimi's face only to be replaced with confused look. No words came out her mouth either.

"Don't you get it, Tony? She is only in it to cause you pain. Where will she be tomorrow when you need somebody to talk to? She won't have time for you. She'll be nowhere around. Tony, you know all this. Why are allowing her to use you?"

Stacy needed Tony to agree with her. If he would only put Mimi out and apologize for being overtaken by her seduction, things could continue to be as they were between the two of them before Mimi entered his bed—entered their bed. Instead, Tony's eyes looked to Mimi. His gaze was saying he wanted her even as Stacy stood in the room begging for his love.

Stacy broke down on the side of the bed. Distress came from the depth of her soul. She cried out for Mimi to leave.

Mimi finally made a move. She sat up and went to hug Stacy.

Tony said that Stacy had it for him in a bad way, but damn girl,' Mimi thought. "Look Stacy, I'm sorry. I didn't mean..."

Stacy snatched away from Mimi and yelled, "You didn't mean what?"

A voice rose out of Stacy's chest that sounded like it came straight from hell. Her narrow eyes revealed a dark shade of evilness that Mimi had never before seen. "To end up like yo' nasty-ass momma? I didn't ask you to give me no damn speech. I simply asked you to tell him the truth. Tell him he won't always be able to come up with enough cash to receive your services. Tell him how you sucked a man's dick in less than twenty seconds for a few dollars. Explain to him like you explained to me that life was all about money."

The look on Mimi's face unveiled all the suffering that accompanied the words Stacy confirmed. If Stacy would have cared enough, she would have heard her friend's heart shatter.

Rage replaced hurt on Mimi face as she spoke, "Sorry to burst your bubble but it was free of charge. See, Tony and me go back a ways, *if* you can recall."

Stacy could hear the fire underneath Mimi's words, so she took fuel to the fire in her own words saying, "Tony, please inform this tramp that you are done with her," Stacy demanded once more. "He doesn't want you!" she yelled at Mimi. "He loves me. Tony please tell her you love me!"

Stacy was upset again, and it was starting to show. Her voice was no longer weak and needy; once again it was angry and powerful.

"Baby, calm down," Tony said in tired tone.

"Don't call me baby. That's not what I want to hear. I want you to tell this streetwalker that she can leave. You and I have some things to discuss."

"Look, I ain't for all this drama. Love ain't never been on my list of things to achieve in life. If he loves you, cool. I don't have to personally hear it. You know it, he knows it. Big fucking deal," Mimi said putting on her clothes. "I got things to do so I'm outta here. Besides, I'm breaking one of golden rules—giving pussy away for free. But I figure it wouldn't hurt since he always had a thing for me."

Mimi knew the last sentence would add salt to Stacy's wound. She deserved it, talking about Latoya.

"You ain't going nowhere, Mimi, not until he tells you he don't want nothing else to do with you."

Both of the women looked at Tony. He flopped down on the bed in his nakedness and refused to repeat the words Stacy demanded to hear. Mimi, tired of the whole scene, grabbed her purse and walked out of the door.

"Why?" Stacy screamed at Tony, "Why did you do this to me? Why are you still bent on having that whore?"

"Maybe it's because I loved her before she was a whore."

"What?" Stacy yelled and started swinging at Tony. At that very moment she wanted him dead. Any death was not good enough; she wanted to rip him apart and kill him with her bare hands.

"Don't tell me this bullshit. I won't hear of this. What did she do? Some whore shit that turned you out that quick? I've seen the bitch working before. You so damn weak that you gonna let her play you that easily?"

Tony grabbed Stacy and held her down. "Stop all this! I'm not gonna let you beat my ass over something you already knew."

Tony was angry and the tone of his voice let Stacy know he was not for anymore of her games. "It was no secret to you how I felt about Mimi. Ain't you the same person I went to when she had me feeling down? Ain't you the one I poured out my feelings to about her breaking my heart? This should be no shock to you. This isn't a shock to you. You, of all people, know how I feel about the *whore*, as you call her.

"I mean, I'm sorry things are the way they are, but damn baby! Stop with all this violence! Stacy, I didn't see us as becoming an item. You did all of this. I'm not blaming the whole ordeal on you, but me coming at you about Mimi wasn't to get at you. It was for advice. You turned it into a relationship. You pushed yourself on me and yea, I could have done better by turning you away. Maybe I thought Mimi would be mad at you and come to me. Maybe I thought she would want to pay you back. Never in a million years did I think you and I would be where we are now. I never expected true feelings to be part of the ordeal. All of this only added more confusion to the picture. I don't know what to say to you about the situation. Stacy, I don't want to lie to you and tell you something just to make you feel better." Tony took a deep breath and lay across the bed.

Stacy threw herself on top of Tony's body and began crying. That truth was this was something she did not know how to handle. The smell of Mimi's sweat on Tony's skin only made her cry harder. "But what about us?" she finally found the courage to whisper. "We can't continue if you are still in love with her."

"Stacy," Tony said in a soft irritated tone, "I never fell out of love with her. I think you always knew that."

17

Sweets (Carry Witherspoon)

She turned the key slowly.

"Hey, daddy!" Sweets yelled as she entered the dark empty apartment. It was her place of peace, a small spot in the big world where she could pretend she was a regular woman and not a whore. She had been looking forward to her visit with the Old Man. Hell, she always looked forward to gracing his presence.

Over the years, he had become a release. Old Man allowed Sweets to be the person she was before she met Dollar Bill. She transformed into the innocent girl who let boys touch on her private parts for satisfaction and not money in a time period when the boys did not call girls names that made fast girls think badly of themselves. The fella doing the touching actually thought the fast girls were nice people, maybe even fantasized about having a fast girl as a girlfriend —until older brothers burst those bubbles sharing that they, too, played with fast girls. Yep, Old Man took Sweets way back.

Sweets opened the door with the key that was given to her years ago by the trick. Old Man was Sweets' best kept secret. He was the only male that she considered part of the human race—well, him and Dollar Bill. As much shit as she talked about men, they were not a part of that equation.

He was a trick Sweets had been seeing for years. He was an easy lay and, over the years, had become a good friend. If tricks could be considered friends, he was as close as one could get. In the beginning of the relationship, he asked her to stop working the streets, made conversation like he wanted to marry her, take her away from the wild side of life. Old Man said he was willing to leave his family, wife and son, to introduce her to a better world.

The pussy-whipped nigga had been married for decades. After a few nights with Sweets, he was willing to forget about the promise he made in his church, to his God, to his wife. Yea, and he was a deacon, more proof to her hypothesis that tricks were not the smartest people on earth. Why would he give up a good churchgoing woman to kick it around town with Sweets, somebody who had fucked damn near his entire congregation?

Sweets turned down his invitation. She could not see herself stuck with an old-ass man who had a thing for old-ass whores. Besides, he was too good for her. Even though she was hard up for money, Sweets knew she could not be faithful to him. Dollar was the only man she was ever true to— in the heart, that is. With him out of the picture, taking another man's last name just would not be right. True, Dollar was dead and gone, never to return, but that still did not stop her from loving him. Trying to put Old Man in his shoes was not going to change the way Sweets felt. It would not even begin to take the sting out of her heart.

She had to admit, though, the old man had a way of making her feel better about the way things were going in her life, yet he lacked the magic Dollar had when it came to loving her like she felt she needed to be loved. Lucky for him, breaking his heart was not in her cards.

'Maybe I am half decent,' Sweets thought after turning the invitation of a worry-free life down. It would not have worked between the two of them anyway. Half the time his dick did not get hard and, due to his heart condition, medications to get it back in action were out of the question. Nowadays, they spent a lot of time talking. They talked about everything, from Sweets' childhood to her Dollar Bill being killed by those crooked-ass cops. Old Man was a release from all the confusion and madness when she had nobody else to let loose on. He had turned into a father figure, if someone could ever figure fucking her own father.

Sweets walked through the living room straight to the bedroom. She did not bother to turn on any lights. She knew the place like the back of her hand. Since he was not there yet, she figured she would wait for him in her birthday suit. He always said his favorite outfit was her flesh and all that other stuff got in the way and hid the natural beauty of a woman. At the sight of her body, his old ass would get all excited and dance around the room making like he had action. After all his hooping and yelling, they would cuddle in the bed and laugh all night. His presence made Sweets feel young again. All her insecure thoughts about gray hair and wrinkles evaporated when he was near.

He had plenty of jokes. Unlike most tricks, his jokes were funny. Sweets would laugh so hard, tears would roll down her face. In addition, none of his jokes were vulgar. He never used bad language in her presence and, if a bad word slipped, he was careful to apologize. Old Man treated Sweets like a woman—something that, through the years, she allowed herself to forget even though she was scared to believe his promises that they could grow old together. He often spoke words that, she felt, came straight from his heart; words that assured her of a beauty she possessed that would never fade in his sight.

Old Man held a truth in his eyes when he spoke of her looks. He made it seem as if she was doing him a favor spending time with him.

"You a special person, and don't even know it," he often said on the verge of tears.

Sweets never let him know she believed any of what he said.

"Old Man, you just horny is all. I ain't nothing to brag about. I'm just a simple ol' whore."

If Sweets did not stop the conversation, she knew she could easily be sucked in. His words made her feel something she had forgotten existed: possibilities. They took her back to a place in life when things were not so complicated, when a man smiling at her saying, "Hello," meant "Have a nice day," in a life when a man rushing to open a door for her did not mean he wanted to find out how to get a cheap quickie.

Sweets did not have to pretend to enjoy Old Man's companionship. She actually did enjoy the time they spent together. With him, she was allowed to be herself and all the acting was put on hold. Had she never got caught up in the street life and fell for Dollar, he was the kind of man she would have liked to marry. Old Man was the only trick Sweets did not share with Mimi.

She lay across the bed in the pitch-dark room, butt-naked, feeling at ease about her living conditions, waiting for him to enter the apartment and erase some of the misery out of her pitiful world.

"You slimy bitch," An unknown voice came out nowhere.

Sweets jumped out of the bed. She did not know what to think.

'Old Man wouldn't set me up,' she thought. They had been sharing this apartment for years. This was their place. No one knew about it.

"What the fuck is going on?" Sweets responded in a shaky tone.

"Your days of fucking my husband are over. I know you thought his limp dick ass would be waiting here for you. Thought he would play in your nasty ass and give you his money, *my money*, and come morning, he would walk through my door smelling like yo' tart ass. Sister, I'm sorry to tell you, but those days are long over."

Sweet's heard a gun cock and her eyes doubled in size. "Please, don't do this."

Before she could run toward the front door she heard a loud bang. Sweets hit the floor. A sharp pain rushed through her chest.

"No God, please. I'm sorry..."

18

Latoya (Walker) Wills

Latoya dialed the number before she could stop herself. Even though it had been a few years since she had spoken to her, lately Big Momma had been on her mind. It was the dream. Latoya kept having the same dream night after night.

Some strange dark-skinned man with deep blue eyes was calling out her momma's name over and over. The man looked so much like herself that it scared her. Latoya had never seen her father but, for some strange reason, she felt he was finally coming to her. She could not help but wonder why he would be coming to her in the form of a dream. If God was sending her a father, why would He wait so long to do it? Now, she did not need a father. She needed one years ago.

Standing on top of a cheap pine casket, this strange man held out his hands, apologizing and screaming Big Momma's name over and over. The first couple of nights, Latoya ignored the dream but after a week of seeing his face and hearing his cries, she decided to give her momma a call. Her husband, Anthony, was at work and Little Man was asleep.

Latoya dialed the number then quickly hung up before the second ring.

What would she say? How would she explain not calling home for the last five years? What if she was needed at home? There was no possible way she could up leave and go see about anything. If she did not know anything bad had happened, she could always use that as an excuse for not coming when she was needed because if something terrible had happened, there was no way she could explain to her new family why she had to leave and go back to a place that they did not know existed.

Latoya walked away from the phone and started her daily chores.

19

Willie Joe Johnson

That girl is a chip off the old block if I should say so myself. I want to get mad at her, but I guess, rightfully, I can't. I was good at walking away from my responsibilities, too. Maybe it's in that new stuff doctors done discovered. What's that they call it, DNA? That girl is so much like me, it's ugly. Sad thing is, it could have all been prevented. I could have stopped the cycle before it began.

Her running off and leaving my grandbaby to the wolves ain't right.

I know it's crazy. Some people may think I got a lot of damn nerve. And I do, but still, you can't judge me for wanting better for mines today; even if I didn't rightfully put a claim on her when I had a chance. I ain't trying to take none of the blame away from myself.

How can you blame a person for wanting more? The world was a different place in my day. Being born a nigga was the worst thing that could happen to a person. Being born a jet-black nigga was even worse than that. After slavery, white folks did not have no use for dark colored niggas. Even during my grandpa's days— slave days —us darkies had to work the fields. They only wanted high-yella niggas in they house and around they children.

And the piss-colored niggas did not make it easy for the dark ones. It was almost like we had two races. Them high-yella colored ones had a way of making dark ones feel less than human and it was worse than when the white folks did it. You would think since they was part of us they'd have some pity. Surely they knew how it felt to not be wanted? Why would they go and make things worse for us? A few treated us nice, but those who weren't nice to us were mean as hell. I mean, even after slavery, one of them light niggas would give dark-skinned people a look that said "Stay the hell away from me!"

They even started up clubs that was just for them. You had to be a certain color to join 'em. No matter how much you had bettered your living situation, making a little money, owning your own plot of land, they still wouldn't let you in. One of them clubs even had a blind man sitting at the door taking a small-tooth comb through everybody's hair. If yo' hair wasn't fine enough to go through that comb, you was not getting through that door. Sounds silly, but it's true.

Then they had another club called The Blue Vein. To get through that door, your skin had to be light enough for your veins to be seen pumping blue blood. Crazy as it sounds, you had folks fussing and screaming about the color of their blood, some folks swearing they veins were colored so they had the right to join the club. No matter how they complained, most didn't get through. Them folks treated us as if we had a choice about what color our skin was. Hell, if we could choose, we would have had one of them slave masters rape our mommas, too. That's how desperate the situation was.

I fed into all the nonsense. Yep, thought I was gonna be the last of my clan to bear the cross. I had to get me something light to prove that I was just as good. Maybe I couldn't enter those high-society places, but my children would and that was good as it would get for me. Told myself, if I could help it, my children wouldn't live though the pain that I did. Rejection wasn't something my children would know about—well, at least not rejection from they own race. If I had anything to do with it, they would be the ones doing the rejecting.

Thinking back, that had to be the reason I allowed my wife and mother-in-law to treat me like a field hand, 'cause anybody with half a cup of sense would have walked 'way from all that madness. Maybe, somewhere deep inside, I wanted yella babies, too. If I could have avoided the mean comments about me being a witch doctor, I would have went along peacefully with all the praying and hoping for anything that wouldn't resemble me. After all, ain't that why I walked away from Big Momma and Latoya?

Guess my only fault is I thought I could skip over the truth to get to the good part of life. In the end, no matter how you cut it, life ain't worth much 'less you honest with yourself.

See, I been coming to that girl in dreams. I know she don't know me. Ain't never seen me a day in her life. Well, she seen me, but didn't know I was her pappy she was staring at. She was with Big Momma coming out of the post office. I looked at that child on Big Momma's hip and, in my heart, knew she was more mines than any of them yella children I had at that miserable place I called home. But what did I do? I kept right on walking like she was a stranger. In a sense, she was 'cause she didn't know to call me, "Daddy."

Now, here I lay in this damn hot box trying to reach out to her.

I know a lot more these days. I guess the Lord put me in a place where my understanding would be better. Crazy thing is, I ain't upset about my predicament. I'm more like grateful. I could have went on over to the other side (whichever side will have me). Instead, I'm here. Oh, I won't lie and tell you it's a nice place. I stay hot and thirsty but my worrying keeps my mind off all that.

I'm grateful that I get a second chance to do what I refused to do when I was alive and kicking. I'm permitted to see my child. I don't know how long I'll be able to come to her in her dreams. Even though she won't listen, I know not to get upset with her for ignoring me. After all, that's what I did to her all my living days. If only I had took the chance to come to her in the flesh, sit her down and talk to her, let her know face to face how sorry I am about my past doings, then maybe I could have instructed her to do what I didn't have the intelligence to do—to go get her baby girl.

20

Mimi Walker

Mimi stood at Sweets' gravesite sobbing like a newborn baby. A large pink marble headstone displayed "Carry Witherspoon" in bold letters. The date of birth and death were written in small letters under the name. Mimi had a picture of Sweets in her younger days wearing a tight blue dress with her head tossed back displaying a big bright smile engraved in the headstone. She knew Sweets would want a headstone that was different, something that stood out. That was the way she lived her life.

The funeral was small. Not many people were willing to reveal that they associated with people like Sweets. So only two people showed up—Mimi and some old man. The old man passed out and had to be carried away before service began. Mimi never got a chance to meet him properly. The service was held at the funeral home. Big Momma did talk one of the deacons at her church into saying a few nice words about Sweets. Right after the service, the deacon left. Mimi rode in the limousine to the gravesite alone. The ride gave her time to try and clear her mind.

After learning of Sweets' death, she went into Sweets' stash and took all the money she had put away for her retirement. Twenty-thousand dollars was the total amount tucked in four mason jars in the far corner under her bed. Mimi spent every penny on a lavish funeral. She put Sweets in the most expensive dress she could find—a five thousand dollar Gucci. The lady who ordered it at the mall did a double take when she found out Mimi was buying the dress for a burial. It was hot pink with slits up both sides and the top was cut low. Mimi knew Sweets would have loved the dress, so she had no second thoughts about her purchase. She could not bear sending Sweets off in some white or black church dress. Mimi figured Sweets would wake up on the other side as a stranger to herself.

'She might get to heaven in a long white gown with a funny hat on and not recognize herself,' Mimi thought while paying for the hot number.

She wanted desperately to get in touch with Sweets' family but, after frantically searching her room for any information that might expose their whereabouts, Mimi gave up. The lack of family in Sweets' life expressed the fact that she had cut them off or, rather, they had cut her off. Dollar Bill was the only family she had and he was long gone. Sweets seemed to have accepted the fact that her difference was something many people could not accept in the light. All of her visits were night visits. The same men who lay in her bed in the wee hours of the night sharing their deepest feelings with her walked right past Sweets in the morning. Her relationships ended with the rising of the sun. Maybe Sweets' family could not accept that.

Sweets had a photo album full of pictures. She had pictures of what looked to be a happy family, aunts, uncles, cousins, friends and more. She never spoke of any of those people Mimi viewed in the pictures. She had never even pulled the photo album out. Mimi ran across it while searching for Sweets' stash. The photos introduced her to a person she never had the chance to meet. Sweets seemed to be so happy in that time of her life. There was innocence about her that Mimi did not know existed. She could not imagine her as a little girl, a girl with no worries about money to say the least. The hardened individual Mimi knew seemed to have no connections with the person in the pictures.

Mimi decided that her favorite picture was the one of Sweets sitting in her daddy's lap on Christmas morning. She looked to be eight or nine in the picture. Her ponytails hung to her shoulders and her smile lit up the aged photo. She seemed to be as happy as a person could possibly be.

'A daddy can do all that?' Mimi thought to herself looking at the photos.

After realizing that she would not be able to contact anyone, she decided to plan the burial ceremony alone. She thought about including Big Momma in the process, but quickly changed her mind. Big Momma would want everything done traditionally and Sweets was not a traditional woman.

"Just when I found me somebody who understands me, you up and leave," Mimi said to the headstone as if Sweets was listening to every word she said.

"I ain't never been much on trusting adults, besides Big Momma, but I did learn to trust you. I never had a doubt in my mind that you didn't have my back. You loved me for me, Sweets. I never told you this, but you were my new momma. I know'd in my heart that you wouldn't abandon me. Yea, I know it was a give and take relationship, but at least we had an honest one. You gave me a solid foundation and some asshole stole it from me. Somebody came and grabbed the ground from under my feet. Now I feel like I'm falling again."

Mimi wiped her face and continued her conversation. "I know you probably upset with me for standing here crying 'cause you was always preaching about being strong. After today, I won't cry no more. After today, I'm gonna find me some solid ground to stand on, even if it's just the memory of what we had." Mimi's teardrops found their way back on her face. "But please don't be mad at me today. My heart is truly broke 'cause I love you. I love you like I used to love my own momma before she up and left me for good. Don't get me wrong, I still love my momma in my mind but I loved you outright. What hurts me the most is that I never got to tell you that. But what comforts me some is the fact that I believe you knew how I felt about you."

Mimi went in her purse and pulled out a piece of paper.

"I wrote something for you," she said, taking deep breath and started to read:

You were my friend. You were my rock.
You will continue to be the voice I hear when I'm lost.
You were all that I thought I never had.
All your teachings, I'll keep like, 'life is too short to live sad.'
Today is the last day I'll cry for you.
You taught me to be strong like the father I never knew.
Not today, but tomorrow, I'll hold your strength so I know you'll excuse me while I cry for you.
But don't get upset. It's only because I love you.

Tomorrow I'll be tough and expose all you have taught me to the world.
Today, let me cry and be weak, reflecting that I'm my momma's little girl.
Goodbye, dear friend. Remember who loved you to the end.
I know you at peace with Dollar Bill again.

Mimi crumbled up the paper and let it fly away in the wind. She knelt down on her knees and kissed the still damp ground. Her tears hit the ground as if they were watering the flowers that were placed on the grave. Without thinking to wipe her face, she got up and started walking.

'Everybody has a true love in their life,' Mimi thought as she walked down the street. Sweets had Dollar Bill and I had Sweets.

'I know Big Momma and Latoya love me but the difference is, they don't understand me. Big Momma has these rules she want me to follow like I was put here to clean up all the mistakes she made in her lifetime. And Momma, I ain't never quite figured her out, yet. All I understand about her is the fact that she don't want me. She never have, let Big Momma tell it. Seemed like I got in the way of her living. Well, not too much in the way 'cause she high-tailed it out of town and left me to fend for myself. Didn't give me no instructions on how to live or nothing. When she did stop through, all she had to tell me was her dream of finding a rich man who would take care of us.

'She never thought to ask me if I wanted my daddy. I don't even know if I want him. She programmed me to hate the nigga before I had a chance to decide for myself. These two and the confusion they pushed in my life. I like to think that I put Sweets' love a step ahead of theirs. Now, look at me. I'm all alone in this fucked-up world. I bet you one thing, Sweets: I won't let it get the best of me.'

Mimi stopped to wipe her eyes and realized she did not have a single tear on her cheeks.

Smiling, she looked up at the sky and said, "I know you proud of me, Sweets."

21

Donald Johnson

Donald knew the time had come to confront Latoya.

"Hello, Latoya," he said entering the nursery of the church during the Sunday School hour.

Latoya sat in the nursery holding a crying baby; she narrowed her eyes when she realized it was Donald who was talking to her. "It would be best if we pretended not to know each other."

Donald laughed.

"Oh, so you playing your role as the preacher's daughter-in-law to the fullest. I understand you don't want his son to find out about Toy— the Toy I used to play with back in the day. I have to admit, I was surprised to find you here of all places. It's been a long time."

"Not long enough," Latoya said sitting the baby down and stepping up to Donald. She decided to say her piece. "You want to talk about us toying around? Well, how 'bout we talk about the baby that came from us doing all that playing. Oh, where'd your slick smile go? Coming up in my church trying to talk crazy to me. Please. Let's talk about you not wanting your high school bride to find out about that baby. Her name is Mimi, by the way."

Latoya stepped back taking in the surprised confusion that overtook Donald's expression.

"What?" Donald exclaimed. A few members passing by paused at the door of the nursery.

"Everything all right?" Sister Gentry asked skeptically looking between the two of them.

Latoya nodded and smiled. Donald cleared his throat and smiled at the ladies who, in turn, shook their heads and walked away.

"I thought you told me that she wasn't mine. I thought we cleared all that mess up years ago," Donald said in a hushed tone.

Latoya rolled her eyes.

"I did clear it up for you. I told you not to worry about it. Donald, I told you what you wanted to hear. Had I told you differently, you would have denied her any way. If my memory serves me right, you deserted me the moment I told you I was pregnant. I refused to have my baby being rejected by the likes of you."

"How you gonna say she's mines? What makes you so sure?"

"Look at you! Still the same big-headed nigga you was in high school. Confidence off the radar, you standing here like you all high and mighty, like yo' shit don't stink," Latoya said scrunching up her nose. "Well, I got news for you. You ain't shit and that bitch of yours ain't shit."

She realized she was in church and decided to slow down and stop before she let things get out of hand or before Mother Wills got wind of her actions.

"Donald, I loved you back then. I thought you loved me, too. Yea, I slept around but I figured we would be back together. Then you had to go get with that silly-ass girlfriend who I see you ended up marrying and here you are acting like you give a damn about being the father of my baby? Please."

Latoya gathered Little Man from the blocks he was playing with on the floor, got up and walked out of the nursery into the hallway that led to the main church lobby. Donald followed slowly behind.

"We shared more than just a one-night stand. The short time we spent together, I was only seeing you. You wouldn't have believed it then and I know you don't believe it now. That's why I just let it all go when you treated me like you did when I told you I was pregnant. But I'll tell you one thing: Mimi looks a lot like that little green-eyed baby girl your wife is carrying around. To be twins, them babies sure don't look nothing alike. Are you sure *those* children are yours?"

"Good evening, Sister Wills," Loretta said to Latoya as she approached the two who had made their way into the church lobby.

Latoya gave her an evil look and walked away without speaking.

"What's wrong, baby?" Loretta asked as Donald turned to stare as

Latoya walked away.

Turning back to her, Donald said, "Nothing, I'm just a little tired from all the overtime I been putting in at the plant."

"Well, maybe you should slow down a bit. I mean, we making it all right. You don't have to work yourself so hard. Me and the twins, we miss having you around on Saturdays."

"I know baby, but we need a few more things and then I'll slow it down."

"Things like what?" Loretta asked, sliding her arm through his as they walked, slowly, through the sanctuary.

"I thought you wanted a new washer and dryer."

Loretta couldn't help but smile. "I said I *wanted* a new washer and dryer. I didn't say I needed a new washer and dryer."

"Same difference," Donald said, returning the smile.

"What was Sister Wills talking about? And what was that look about?" Loretta asked, changing the conversation suddenly. "Seems to me, you two were having a serious conversation."

"Huh, oh, we wasn't talking about much. She was asking me how we like it here and telling me how glad she was we chose this congregation."

"Oh," Loretta said in an 'I Don't Believe You' tone.

"That's weird," she continued. "She hasn't said two words to me. Come to think of it, she seems to be avoiding me. The other day in Bible class, I asked her about a verse and she walked off like she didn't hear me.

"She looks familiar, like I've seen her before. I can't quite put my finger on it. Now, here you are standing in my face telling me she is interested in how you are taking to the church?"

"Baby, she married to the Reverend Wills' son. If she was trying to get at me, do you think it would take place right under her father-in-law's nose?"

"Who said anything about her trying to get at you?"

"You did."

"No, I didn't."

"Oh," Donald said, mimicking Loretta's voice.

"Shut up and let's go find a seat. Service is about to start."

Donald sat in church trying to make some sense out of all the confusion that was just dumped on his world.

'I have a daughter,' he thought. 'She would have to be damn-near grown by now.'

He looked down at Harmony and quickly turned away.

'How was I supposed to know anything about her? First, Latoya told me she was pregnant, and then she told me not to worry about it. Not long after that, she quit school and I never saw her again. How can she blame me for any of this? I was just a child myself. If there is a baby, where the hell is she?'

The whole situation was making Donald's head ache. In his frustration, he stood up.

"Where are you going?" Loretta asked.

"I'm going to step out for a minute. I need some fresh air."

"All right," she said worried.

Donald walked through the church staring disapprovingly at Latoya until he stepped out of the church doors. He sat on the steps and took a deep breath.

The morning air did nothing to stop his head from spinning. Of all places to find out he had an illegitimate child: the church? Really? It gave a hell of a meaning to the saying, "God is gonna get you."

Donald did not know how to feel about this daughter of his — if she even was his daughter. He knew he loved Harmony unconditionally. As a man and her father, it was his duty to protect her from the type of young boys he used to be, a boy who was waiting in the dark to take her into his uncaring arms. It was the same way Donald did Latoya many years ago. True enough, back then, he would have walked away from his child, but only because he did not know any better.

Now, as a man, things were different. All the growing he had done had taught him the importance of virtue. All he had told Loretta before she gave him a second chance was not an act. He meant all he said about growing up and not letting her down. How would she handle this? She could not possibly count this as something he did intentionally. All the days of hurting her were in the past. Donald came to Loretta as a man, not a boy. She had to understand this was a mistake he made before he came and begged her into his life for good.

"I'm sorry you had to find out like this."

Donald turned to see Latoya standing on the steps of the church. For the first time since seeing her, she resembled her old self. She stood on the top step looking like an angel, her white gloves nervously rubbing together. Her sky-blue pleated dress might have hung past her ankles, but the dress still could not hide the fact that her knees were shaking. She carried the same look she wore the night she told Donald she was with child. It was a sad, confused look and the fright in her heart made her eyes look a dull green —not the same illustrious gray he remembered them to be.

"Where is she?" he asked.

"Home...with Big Momma," Latoya managed to say.

"Are you sure she's mines?"

"Please don't ask me that again. If I was intending to trick her off on you, don't you think I would have gotten more out of you back then?"

"When can I see her?"

"You can't!" Latoya almost leapt off the steps.

"What?" Donald stood up and faced Latoya with a look of death in his eyes. "How the hell you gonna tell me I got a child, then in the same breath tell me I can't see her? You need to stop with the bullshit, Toy."

"Look Donald, you done fucked up my life once. I don't need you to do it again. These people here don't know nothing about Toy. They only know about Latoya. My past is one I created. My present is something I created, and Mimi ain't in it."

Donald could not believe what he was hearing. He balled his right fist and punched at the air. Through clenched teeth, he managed to say, "You mean to tell me you erased your child out of your history? Latoya, that ain't possible. You can't just pretend she don't exist."

"You did," Latoya said rolling her eyes.

"That's not fair."

"Oh, so you think it was fair for me? I made me a life and I don't need you or nobody else coming around messing things up for me. I don't need you or your wife's permission to do a damn thing. These people around here gave me the space I needed to change, something those small-minded folks back home wouldn't allow me to do."

"What has that got to do with your child, your own flesh and blood?"

"Well, look who is being judgmental." Latoya cocked her head to the side. "The same nigga who didn't even want to take time out to claim her. Well, shame on me for up and leaving her, but what do we say about the nigga who refused to even acknowledge her? Now, I might allow my momma to talk down to me or anybody else from that godforsaken place we call home, but buddy, you don't have room."

"Big Momma still stay in the same place?" Donald said, ignoring Latoya's comment

"Why?" Latoya's voice got shaky.

"Look, you crazy-ass woman, either you tell me where Big Momma is residing or I'll walk up to Reverend Wills and tell him all about us growing up together."

Latoya stared at Donald with a blank look in her eyes. All of her color seemed to have disappeared.

"Look Latoya, you may be right about a lot of the things you said to me. Still, that don't stop me from wanting to meet her. I just want to see her. Back then, I was a bigheaded boy, but people change and today, right now, you speaking to a grown-ass man. I don't know what I'm gonna say to her. I can't begin to make up for abandoning her, but one thing she will know: from here on out, she ain't gotta do nothing by herself. I won't tell her nothing about you. To be honest, I don't even know how she'll fit into my world, but I'll give *her* the option of turning me down."

"Yea, Big Momma still on Tyler Street." Latoya heard the words, but didn't quite believe she gave the answer. "Promise me you won't mention none of this to these people around these parts. Donald, you got a life. You got a wife and twins. Besides, you a man. God made things easier for you. Y'all get to do all the picking. It's not easy for a middle-aged woman to try and find a husband. Don't mess it up for me. This was my one chance to make a good clean start."

Donald walked back into the building without responding to Latoya.

22

Big Momma

Big Momma grinned i spite of herself.

"I sho' do miss having you around. I miss talking to you. I ain't got nobody to cook for. After cooking big meals all these years, my food just don't taste right when I try to section it off and make smaller helpings. Mimi, now that you by yourself, why don't you consider coming back home?"

Mimi had thought plenty of times about moving back home, but she knew her lifestyle would not fit into Big Momma's house. She steered their conversation back to a safe place by talking about food.

"Well, by the taste of these dumplings, I can't tell the difference. Big Momma," Mimi said after scooping the last spoonful of dumplings into her mouth, "you know I can't move back with you. You know as well as I do you ain't gonna put up with strange men calling and pulling up to your front door yelling my name."

"Well, you think you could have them meet you on the corner?"

Mimi laughed. "I ain't gonna be walking to no corners to meet nobody. That's how I used to do it when I was sneaking off doing wrong in the dark. Nowadays all my wrongdoing takes place in the light."

"Child, you gonna be the death of me, yet."

" 'Cause you love me too much."

"What?"

"I said you love me too much. Maybe if you learn to love me like a granddaughter instead of a daughter, I wouldn't cause you half the problems."

Big Momma started to get upset with Mimi's comment but instead she had to take it for what it was worth—the simple truth.

"Well, baby, God didn't leave me much of a choice now did He? If

I ask you something, promise me you'll tell me the truth and not worry about my feelings."

"Promise," Mimi said, crossing her arms and laying them on the kitchen table looking Big Momma in the eyes.

"Did I love you enough?"

"Big Momma, you gave me plenty love. I…" Mimi got quiet and turned away.

"Don't go getting quiet on me now. You promised me the truth and that's what I intend to hear."

"I just wanted her love, too." Mimi stared into space. "No matter what you did, it wasn't gonna amount to what she was supposed to do. She was my momma. Being so young, I didn't know it was possible to live and be happy without her. Not relying on my feelings, I've managed to avoid a lot of heartache. You may have deeply disliked Sweets, but she taught me that much."

"Baby, it's not a good thing to go through life not using your feelings. That just ain't healthy." Big Momma walked across the room and grabbed her and held her in her arms.

"Nah, Big Momma, you misunderstanding me." Mimi laid her head on Big Momma's chest for the first time in many years. "I do use my feelings. I haven't turned them completely off. I love you, I love Momma and Lord knows I loved Sweets, God rest her soul. I won't just hand over my emotions to any man. I'm not gonna sit here and say no man will ever get through to my heart, but I will say I ain't looking. He's gonna have to find me, and prove a hell of a whole lot to me.

"Big Momma, in my profession I see men for what they truly are. More than half of my clients are married; they own wives don't even know them. These wives are living with strangers. I know more about they sexual habits than the women they married. With they wives, they pretend. With me, they let loose and enjoy the night. As a prostitute, I got a third eye. The devil may have given it to me but I can see a man better than the average woman."

"Well, it sounds like you gonna have it a lot easier than me or yo' momma 'cause, at one point, we believed anything a man ever told us. But all those strange men you have taken to lying around with? Child, that part I'll never understand. Still, you my grandbaby so I have no choice but to love you. Lord knows I truly hate what you do."

"Big Momma, it ain't as bad as you think it is. It's just a job like yours or anybody else's."

"Mines? I ain't never laid in bed..." Big Momma said pulling away from Mimi and sitting back down at the table.

"Big Momma, you remember how you used to come home from work fussing about all the pretending you used to have to do for them nasty-ass folks in them nasty-ass rooms you cleaned? Or when you worked at the grocery store and you had to pretend not to be bothered by dumb folks who couldn't count but who was talking down to you? That's all I do. I lay around pretending these nasty men are turning me on. Most of them is so horny, they cum before they even get they clothes off."

Big Mama raised a swift hand in the air to cut Mimi off.

"Child, don't you ever go into details like that with me again."

"Sorry, Big Momma," Mimi said laughing.

"I'm not playing with you. You wanna be barred from my house again?"

"No, Big Momma, I won't ever give you details again."

"Thank you, child. Now help me out by cleaning up this kitchen."

"All right."

Mimi carefully washed the good dishes and put the leftover dumplings in a to-go bowl. After mopping the floor, she headed to Big Momma's room. There, she found Big Momma sitting in a chair holding a picture of Latoya when she was all of five-years-old.

"We look like twins," Mimi said interrupting Big Momma's thoughts.

"Yep, look so much alike, I just knew God had given me a brand-new start."

"Everybody got a different soul, Big Momma. People don't see or feel things the same. It's kind of like me taking a liking to your dumplings but, Momma, she would rather you fry her up some chicken. We look the same on the outside but our insides are different. It ain't nothing you did. It just the way we was made. Big Momma, stop blaming yourself."

"I hear all you say but, Mimi, you ain't never had a child. You don't know the feeling of not knowing her well-being. At times, I find myself wondering if she's dead. Plenty of nights, I done cried myself to sleep wondering if I missed her funeral. I would hate for her to be sent to her maker alone. It wasn't right that you had to do all that for Sweets. Her momma should have buried her."

Silence overtook the room for a few seconds.

"If only she would call or give me a signal telling me she's all right. Hell, she could call and hang up in my face just as long as she let me know she's alive."

Mimi took the picture from Big Momma's hands, led her to the bed and sat her down. "Big Momma, Momma is where she wants to be. She been running for a long time since I can recall. What she wants out of life ain't never been here so she took to getting away. I've come to realize the only reason she stayed around as long as she did was on account of me. Even I wasn't enough to hold her down or to give her roots. You did your part. You raised her and loved her. But you can't live her life. Wherever she is, she is happy as she is gonna be but, to be honest with you, I don't think she is ever gonna be happy."

"What makes you think you know so much, child?"

"Because when I was a child, I watched my momma. I lay in the bed with her and watched her eyes change colors while she told me her dreams of, one day, taking me away from this place. We shared everything. I know the pattern of her heartbeat. I know the scent of her skin before and after a session of lovemaking with a strange man. We shared the same dirty brown bath water while she made promises of giving me a better life.

"She didn't know but I figured out why we always took the long way home. I knew she was avoiding all the stares that came with holding my illegitimate hand. She never made me stay home. All I had to do was cry and she held her hand out and in the sweetest voice called to me, 'Come on here.'"

Mimi took a deep breath before she continued. "See, Big Momma, you were so worried about my daddy that you being mad at her blocked all that was in plain sight, even to a little child. You ever notice how she walked with her head down instead of high in the air like it was supposed to be? Or the sad look that would appear on her face when she saw a young couple with children? Even how easy she cried when a love scene was playing on TV?

"Momma was looking for love in the strangest places. It seemed to me that she thought maybe love would come as a surprise in a box of cereal. Looking back on it all, it doesn't shock me that she believed all the lies those men were telling her each time she left. Big Momma, it had nothing to do with you. We all choose who we want to love. You chose to love your child unconditionally and, Momma, she chose to love love."

Big Momma wiped the tears from her eyes. "You did know her better than me."

"No, I wouldn't say all that. I would say I knew a different part of her. I don't know her first words or when she took her first steps. To be honest, here lately, I just been putting everything together. I didn't understand her when I was growing up. I spent the first half of my life being in love with her and the next part of life mad at her for leaving me. It wasn't 'til Sweets that I started trying to figure her out. Sweets made me realize you can't fault people for how they are. I think maybe I just knew her in a different way than you did."

"That damn Sweets wasn't all that bad."

"No, Big Momma she wasn't. She was really a good person. Given a different profession, you two could have been good friends."

"Yea, given a different profession. Speaking of friends, whatever happened to that Stacy girl? I see she still around here. All them grand dreams of her daddy sending off to some big college didn't make it past his front yard."

Mimi's whole disposition changed at the mention of Stacy's name.

"She still around," Mimi mumbled. "We just don't see eye to eye anymore."

"Oh, she don't approve of how you living your life?"

"Something like that," Mimi lied.

"Oh well, it took some time for me to come around. You can't just push the new you off on people. Give it some time, she'll come around. You spending the night with me?" Big Momma asked slipping into her nightgown.

"If you'll have me."

"Have I ever had a choice?"

"Nope, scoot over. Tonight I'm sleeping with you."

"Don't go gettin' fresh with me. I'm still pretty good with my left hook."

"Oh Big Momma, you love me too much to be fighting on me. Besides, we shared tonight. Our emotions have been overworked. Tears make you tired. I know you don't have the energy to be swinging on me. Forgive me for my slip of the tongue." Mimi cuddled in a soft meaty spot on Big Momma's back and went fast to sleep.

For the first time in a long time she did not dream. She rested.

23

Stacy Williams

Stacy rolled over in bed and hit the alarm clock. Five in the morning was not her ideal time of getting her day started. Things had changed a lot since she allowed Tony to enter her world. All the plans her father had of her attending a top-notch college seemed to disappear with the appearance of Tony. Now she was stuck in this nowhere-ass town working part-time as a sales clerk in an expensive plus size store. No matter how hard she tried, she couldn't get excited about school.

Stacy could not even pretend anymore—pretend for her father, pretend for her teachers, not even for herself. Whenever she opened a book, the words seemed to blur together. How she was able to walk across the stage and receive a diploma still amazed her. Thinking back, she could not remember a single assignment she turned in her last semester of school. The teachers had to feel sorry for her because she wore her emotions on her sleeve, the same way Mimi said Latoya wore hers.

Stacy felt right at home at her new job though. It kept her busy and left her no time to think about Tony or Mimi. The place was always full of snobby overweight women. It required no thinking, just a bunch of smiling and lying. "Yes, that looks real good on you," she repeated all day to overweight women who pranced around in dark colors with pinstripes.

She sold decorated high-priced curtains labeled as dresses to these mean, rude, fat women. Light colors were not an option for the elephant-sized bodies that frequented the store. Sure, some outfits had a little pink and yellow in the fabric here and there, but the base colors were always bark-brown, ash-gray or jet-black. Even the lighting was dim in the department store as if they were hiding the women in plain sight.

It was the just environment Stacy needed for the mess she had created. After breaking in on Tony and Mimi, and making an ass out of herself, Tony stopped seeing her. All the begging, pleading and crying in the world would not make him change his mind and reconsider taking her back. Stacy got so bad, Tony's mother actually called her father and asked him to put a stop to her calling and crying at all times of the day and night. Mr. Williams was not only upset, but also shocked because Stacy was not supposed to be dating until after college. College, then boys was what he always drilled in her head. It did not matter, though. Stacy had ruined the order of things.

Mr. Williams went to Stacy and demanded that she stop seeing Tony. Stacy was desperate and did not stop even after her father's warning. Tony's rejection only made her try harder.

How could he forget all the special moments they shared? What could possibly make him turn away from her so easily? He had to mean it when he said he loved her.

There was no way anybody could fake what they we shared,' she thought.

Stacy started waiting around for him at school, following him to his classes. She felt all he needed was to listen to her then he would see things her way. But, instead of him listening, the teachers got involved by calling her parents and informing them of her skipping classes. Through that process, they pulled up her grades that she had been able to hide all that time due to her unpaid fees.

Stacy thought her father was going to kill her in the principal's office. Instead, he waited until they got home and whipped her for the first time in years. He threatened to have her sent away until her mother stepped in.

"College is out of the question!" he yelled. "Either find her a job or she's getting the hell out of my house!"

Stacy's mother knew he meant every word that came out of his mouth. Two weeks after graduation, Stacy found herself working at Sabrina's Plus Sizes for Special Women. A year after graduation, Mr. Williams still was not speaking to her. He gave his usual morning and evening greetings, but nothing more.

It was more than evident Mr. Williams' heart was broken. He had poured all his dreams into his daughter. He planned and saved for a future that did not include any type of service work. It was her education that prevented him and his wife from moving away to a better neighborhood and splurging on expensive household appliances. Mr. Williams had put money up for his daughter's education. His baby girl was to have letters in front of her name. He wanted his daughter to be the topic of the dinner table discussion.

Instead, Stacy had chosen to ruin that, to embarrass him to no end. No longer did he brag about her to coworkers or family members. Nowadays, he got upset when her name was mentioned. She threw everything he did for her away.

"Stacy," Mrs. Williams said entering her room.

"Yes, Momma?"

"You need to be getting yourself together. You don't want to miss your bus."

"I'm up, Momma."

"Yea, but you need to be moving. Let's not give your father something else to complain about."

"Momma, will he ever forgive me?"

"In time. It's just that he expected a lot more out of you. I expected a lot more out of you. You still my baby so I'm going to work with you."

Stacy moved slowly. The warmth of the bed was not something she was looking forward to leaving. After finally accepting the fact that Tony was not a choice, Stacy realized she wanted a change. School would put excitement into her daily routine and give a reason to get up in the morning. She did not know how to approach the topic with her parents.

True, her mother might agree with her, but her father would be footing the bill. His treatment made her question if he even loved her anymore.

"Momma," Stacy said softly, "you know, I can still go to college. Maybe it won't be a college he wants me to attend. I been thinking about a community college around here."

Mrs. Williams looked doubtful.

"Momma, I know you don't think I can do it, but I know I can. I'm not talking about right now; I'm talking more like next year. I know I'll have to pay for it myself, but if Daddy lets me stay here, I know I can do it."

A smile quickly spread over her mother's face.

"Why not right now? Why you want to wait a semester? I know he don't act like it, but he still dreams of you moving ahead. He didn't spend all those extra nights away from home driving that truck so you would end up like us. All he has ever talked about was you becoming an independent woman. All he wanted was you to make a life for yourself.

"Baby, you broke your daddy's heart by giving up on school. You couldn't have done no worse than by getting pregnant. Life is hard for a woman and double hard for a black one."

Stacy caught her Mom's infectious smile and grinned for the first time in weeks.

"Momma, I'm gonna go back. I just need to clear my head, get some things straight. If I was to go to school now, it would be for Daddy and not me. I don't think I would do very well."

"Well, I'll tell you one thing Ms. Confused, you better get it together quick, fast and in a hurry. I don't know how much longer he's gonna be able to stand you sitting around sulking over a boy who don't want you. It's best you wake up and smell the coffee. While you sniffing, you need to know you can't make nobody love you. Love ain't created unless you created it, like I did you. Love is just there. So while you wondering what you could have, should have, and—given the chance—will do different, try to know sometimes it's not your fault. Life isn't about what you want all the time. More than most, it's about what you need."

Stacy looked at her mother in a different light for the first time. Those were words that sounded like they were coming out of Mimi's mouth, not her mother's.

Mrs. Williams had always been the calm type, never speaking too quickly, always thinking before she opened her mouth, careful not to offend anyone. That day, Stacy was introduced to a new woman. She looked into the early-morning light to get a good look at the person standing in front of her. She needed to make sure it was her mother. Yep, it was her all right—the same caring face; only it sported a new set of eyes. They were stern, informing Stacy that she needed to wake up. Mimi's eyes had the same look the night they fought over Tony. Mrs. Williams was caught between a rock and a hard place — caught between the dream love of her daughter and harsh love of her husband.

'She's right,' Stacy thought. 'I have to do better than this.'

"Ok Momma, I'll start school next semester and I'll do good."

Mrs. Williams breathed a sigh of relief, grabbed Stacy, hugged her and whispered in her ear, "I'll tell him of your new plans and you can quit this job as soon as class starts."

24

Mimi Walker

Sunday was Mimi's true day of rest. No grinning and lying about how good it was. No strange man's sweat mixed in hers. Best of all, no hot-stank breath blowing up her nostrils. Sunday made life normal for Mimi. Just like regular working people, she had something to look forward to—a day off.

Usually, Mimi spent Sundays at Big Momma's house eating dumplings and sweet potato pie. Today, she did not feel like hanging out with Big Momma. Today she wanted a real friend, somebody more her age to laugh with and talk with. How Sweets did it alone still amazed Mimi. Dollar Bill's love had to be something special because that is what Sweets was thriving on after all those years. She managed to live off the memory of what he was.

Mimi pulled her money out of the dresser and recounted $10,000. She had enough money to take a long vacation. What fun would a vacation be if she had no one to take with her? Stacy was the only friend she ever had and she went and fucked that up.

Mimi was still hurt behind Stacy's words. What did Latoya have to do with any of what happened between her, Tony and Stacy?

Of all the people to badmouth her momma, Stacy was the last person Mimi expected to do it. "Friends" was the key word. They were supposed to be best friends. Did they not have a past that was longer than Tony's dick?

Sweets always told her that square chicks let dick get the best of them. Mimi always thought Stacy was different, but so much for that thought. Still, she never imagined Stacy would use her momma as a stepping stone. Stacy knew Mimi's past. She knew all the pain that lived there and, yet, she still did what every other person tried to do—use the painful truth to break Mimi down.

Crazy thing is, Tony didn't want her and she didn't want him. Why Stacy pushed up on him like that she'd never understand.

Days like today, though, Mimi longed for Stacy's conversation. She wanted somebody who understood her feelings without words being spoken. Mimi needed that certain someone who understood her and was not around for just how she could please them. She slowly put her money in her dresser and lay across the bed. Closing her eyes, she promised herself she would not cry. As soon as she closed them, tears fought their way to the surface of her lids.

An image of her momma appeared. Latoya looked as she always did when they lay in the bed together—sad and needy. All the promises her mother told her took over her mind. Promises of a house, a father, and the one that broke Mimi's heart the most—the promise of taking her with her. "You are stronger than this," Mimi said wiping the tears.

"You left your door unlocked," a voice said.

Mimi quickly changed her expression. "What brings you around these parts?"

"Oh, I was just in the neighborhood and thought I'd check on you."

"In the neighborhood my ass. You and that wife-to-be of yours live clear cross-town. Don't think 'cause I don't run in your circle, I don't know what's going on. Big Momma told me soon as she saw it in the church bulletin."

"So you *have* heard the news."

Mimi patted the bed signaling for Tony to come have a seat. "I won't bite you, unless you want me to."

Tony came and sat next to her. He was the somebody she needed. No matter what Mimi did, Tony treated her with respect.

"So, Big Momma filled you in on my wedding."

"Yea, she's mad at you, too."

"Mad at me?" Tony asked confused.

"Yea. She swears up and down that Lisa ain't no good for you. Said you was what I needed to straighten me out."

They both broke out in deep laughter.

"Well, maybe I'll have a talk with her next Sunday and inform her that it was *you* who didn't want *me*."

"Wouldn't do that if I was you. You must have forgotten about her pistol-packing days. It's been rumored that a church house won't stop her from shooting."

"You got a point. I bet she's got a better aim, so I'm gonna leave that alone."

Mimi and Tony laughed until tears came to their eyes. This was the feeling she needed— the feeling of unpolluted pleasure that Tony provided that moment for her. Somehow while laughing, Mimi found herself wrapped in Tony's arms. She placed her hand in the midsection of his back, the area he always instructed her to massage after a session of lovemaking.

"Do you love her?"

'Damn! I'm sounding like Stacy,' Mimi thought.

"No," Tony said with all seriousness.

"No?" Mimi repeated confused.

"She's pregnant."

"Oh." Mimi's hand stopped moving.

"I have to do the right thing. I know she loves me. I think she got pregnant on purpose, but it's too late to debate all that. All I know is that I'm going to be a daddy. The way I see it, daddy adds up to being a father."

"That's a good thing. Children need fathers. If I had a father, maybe I wouldn't be what I am today."

Tony placed his chin on Mimi's head.

"You are a good person, Mimi, you just don't know it. There is more to you than lying up. I won't go off into preaching 'cause I done told you a million times but, I will say, when you do decide to settle, you are gonna make some man happy."

"So since you getting married, does that mean we won't be able to be together anymore?" Mimi looked up at him.

"I told you I don't love her," Tony said flashing a mischievous grin.

Mimi smiled and felt a bit relieved. "Good, 'cause I was just lying here thinking I needed to spend time with a friend."

"Well, I'm here, baby."

PART 4

25

Latoya (Walker) Wills

Latoya sat on the porch wondering where her life was headed. It seemed all the lies she had told were about to come to a head. Why did she tell Donald about Mimi on those stairs at church? She thought telling him would make him leave her alone, thought it would help keep her secrets in the dark.

Donald was not the same selfish person he used to be. He actually wanted to see Mimi and get a chance to judge for himself if she was his daughter. Why would he risk losing his family over a daughter that might not be his? Was he happy with Loretta? Why would he bring unnecessary pain into Loretta's world?

Latoya shook her head in disgust.

'I just can't get away from all the bullshit,' she thought.

Donald was bound to tell Loretta and Loretta was bound to tell the members of the church.

'Something else for the folks back home to laugh about.'

A "Hey there, lady," interrupted her thoughts.

Limping her way was the man in her dreams. He looked older in real life, but he had that same film of sweat covering his body. Latoya shot up and turned to head back to the house quickly.

"No, you don't," he said, smiling, causing her to pause. Fear gripped Latoya.

"Please, don't come near me," she said, turning back around to him with a trembling voice. "I don't know you."

"You know me all right. Well, let's just say this ain't the first time you done laid eyes on me." The blue-eyed, extremely dark-skinned man continued to walk toward Latoya until he was standing on the porch steps right next to her.

"What is it you want with me? Why do you insist on bothering me? Why are you here?" Latoya's voice was unsteady and nervous.

"Well, I reckon it's 'cause you refuse to listen to me in your dreams. Latoya, the Lord has allowed me to try and make right what I made wrong many years ago. Yet, you showed me how hardheaded I was 'cause you done me just like I done you—pretended I didn't exist. But the buck gotta stop somewhere. It seems to me this is as good as any place to start—with me and you."

Latoya looked at the man in disbelief. "What the hell are you talking about? Look, if you don't leave right this minute, I'm gonna call the police on you crazy old man."

"You don't know me," Willie Johnson said. "Yea, you right about that, but I know you. Listen to what I'm about to say before you go running calling the laws"

Willie took a deep breath before continuing his conversation.

"Latoya, you good at doing what's right for you. Your version of 'right' is what you wanna do, never mind the problems it causes everybody else. All this running around, leaving your baby girl to fend for herself? What you doing ain't no good for nobody, not even you. What you doing is only causing more harm to your well-being."

Latoya took a step back, crossed her arms, sucked her teeth and said, "Who are you to come sit on my porch and tell me about my life? You think you know me 'cause of what you done heard? You probably just like the rest of them who think 'cause I been around the block a few times that ain't no good left in me. Well, I got news for you, stranger. I'm a damn good person. I've paid long enough for them foolish mistakes I made as a child. I have found my peace. I'm happy now. I got me a life and I'm not willing to give it up, not even for my baby girl. Besides, she's almost grown. What good will I do her now?"

"Grown, my tail. That child is a lost puppy. She won't find happiness until you go and explain it to her."

"Well, didn't nobody show me any happiness. I had to go out and find it for myself. And who sent you here to ruin my life?"

The blue-eyed man turned his back on her, leaning on the porch rail.

He used what seemed to be most of his energy to yell at the top of his lungs. "Who you think you are 'cause you damn show ain't fooling me! Happy is the last thing you is. Envious of this family you pretending to be part of, mad at them folks back home for not accepting you, holding on to the past for no good reason.

"They say what won't kill you will only make you strong but I do believe it done drove you stark mad!" The man covered in sweat sat down on the porch steps and lowered his voice. "But happy? Nah, you still ain't reached that part of your life, yet. And you wouldn't know a peace-of-mind if it was standing in your living room."

Tears rolled down Latoya's eyes as she started trying to explain herself. This man was revealing so much of her life to her. Still, she was not ready to accept his truth, her truth. "You don't understand." Latoya's voice was almost a whisper. "Here, I'm loved. My husband loves me..."

"Child, your husband don't even *know* you. What you did was wrong, making up a past for that man to believe. You made up a life and a person. You never gave that man a chance to decide if he wanted to love you. You made a past so heartbreaking that he had no choice but to take you in. Ever stop to think the past you ran from might have been enough to make him fall for you? One thing I can tell you from experience, if he loves you like you think he do, he'll move Heaven and Earth to be with you no matter where you came from.

"You being raped and had by more than your share of boys back home won't be enough to keep him away. I know 'cause I did it—did it for all the wrong reasons but, nevertheless, I did it. Funny thing is, you might not want him after you been liberated but you'll never know what liberation is if'n you keep living this made-up story."

Latoya slowly sat down beside him.

"How do you know so much about me?" she asked eyeing him suspiciously.

"Stop pretending, Latoya. You knew who I was that first night I came to you in your dreams. You just decided to blow me off and pretend that I never came to you."

Latoya looked into his face and saw herself— the same dark skin, funny-colored eyes, and naturally wavy hair. A weak feeling crept over her. She thought she had thrown her weakness away once she was married.

All of a sudden, a flood of feelings crashed into her. Tears poured down her face.

"Why did you leave me, Daddy?" she sobbed.

The word, "Daddy," sounded strange coming out of her mouth and felt foreign rolling off of her tongue. Was it not foreign? It was like trying to pronounce the Spanish words in her tenth grade, sixth-hour class; words that she easily learned the meaning of in her head, but did not feel the pronunciation was important. Besides, after the class, she would never say any of the words again.

"If you had been here, then none of those things would have happened to me. I needed you there to protect me. I cried for you almost every night after that Joe Parker did those things to me. I was still a child and, in my heart of hearts, no matter what Momma said about you, I knew you would come and make him pay for what he did." Latoya got quiet and let the tears roll down her eyes. "But you never came. I needed you back in them days, but I don't need you no more."

"True," Willie Johnson answered. "All you said about me is true. Me coming and judging you don't add to a hill of beans considering what I did for you, but you not doing this for me. You doing this for your baby. You need to be a better person than I was. Why would you leave your baby girl hurting the way you was left? You know first-hand how cruel this world is and how it likes to eat the young and pretty up. It chews them around then spits what's left of them out.

"Now what you feel about me is right. I'm not here to defend myself but two wrongs ain't nowhere near right. So, what you gonna do about your problem? I did leave you with a mother. You, on the other hand, done run off and left that child completely alone. Don't even fix your mouth to say Big Momma, 'cause she ain't a momma."

Willie Johnson crept off the porch and headed down the street.

Latoya yelled, "Daddy!" She had so many questions to ask him. Wanted to know more about this man Big Momma always barked and complained about. All her childhood feelings of abandonment simply vanished. A new emotion entered her world, one she could not quite describe other than it was an emotion that was part joy and some pain. But this new emotion offered opportunity.

Having a father meant having a family, which meant having a chance—a chance to belong. For the first time in her life, Latoya felt complete and whole.

"Daddy, please come back! I only want to talk!"

The image of Willie Johnson vanished before her eyes.

26

Donald Johnson

The ride to Big Momma's house was not a long one. Actually, it was too short. All the time in the world would not be enough for Donald to figure this mess out. The one thing he did know was that he was going to give it a try. After explaining it all to Loretta, he felt a lot better. She made it clear that she did not know how to accept the transformation that was about to take place in her family. She did what Donald expected she would do: cried for a few days, kept him from touching her, called him a bunch of well-deserved names, and then they talked about it.

Donald told her if it was going to end their marriage, he would leave it alone. He also reminded her of him having a brother who passed away. The inability to bond with his sibling left a soft spot in his heart for his long-lost baby girl. Still, ignoring it did not change the fact that he had another daughter. Last of all, he explained to his wife, with tears in his eyes, that he wanted to meet his child and make her a part of his existence and him a part of her existence.

Donald left the fate of their marriage up to Loretta.

Driving back home, he still did not know if it was the tears or all the churchgoing that made Loretta agree to him going to meet Mimi. Whatever it was, he was grateful for her willing to accept his child.

Donald took a deep breath before stepping on Big Momma's porch. He was not sure how Big Momma would handle him coming uninvited to her home. Growing up, she was never known to be a friendly woman. Well, back then, she had no right to be with all those boys running in and out of her home until Latoya became pregnant. After that, all of the visits to that sad off-white house stopped. Nothing about the house had changed over the years other than his intention for entering. He actually was coming for Big Momma this time instead of plotting on how to get his hands on her daughter.

He gathered his nerves and knocked on the door again.

Maybe this isn't the right thing to do. Maybe I should have gone to a pay phone and called before coming unannounced. It's not every day that somebody walks into a home to inform somebody that they may be the father of a child,' he told himself and turned away.

"How may I help you?" Big Momma said standing in the door with her hand on her hip, looking irritated.

"Well," Donald said in a nervous tone, "I didn't meant to bother you but I wanted to talk to you about Mimi, if you don't mind."

With the mention of Mimi's name, Big Momma's eyes bulged and her once irritated face turned real mean. "Mimi?" She almost shouted Donald off the porch. "I hope you ain't one of them—what's that she calls y'all?—tricks coming 'round here. I'm not with all that mess.

"She's my grandbaby. You may see her coming to and leaving this house, but don't none of that funny mess take place around here. I'm a decent churchgoing woman and I will call the law on you if you ever show yo' nasty, trifling face around these parts again!"

"Tricks?" Donald stood staring at this oversized woman with a worn out wig on, who looked to have swallowed the old Big Momma he remembered years ago. "Big Momma, I'm no trick. I may be Mimi's father."

"Father?" Big Momma yelled and put her hand to her heart. All this commotion was just about enough to make her have the "big one."

"Yes, father. At least that's what Toy, I mean Latoya tells me."

"You spoke to Latoya?" she asked throwing the screen door wide open.

"Yes."

"Come on in, child. I'm sorry about the misunderstanding. We have a lot to talk about," Big Momma said, opening the door and leading Donald toward the living room.

"Why did you wait so long to come to my grandbaby?" she asked before he took a seat.

"I just found out about Mimi not too long ago. I'm not gonna lie and pretend this is the first I heard of the child but, believe me when I say it's complicated. Now that I know of her, I come to see if she's mines. I know she's almost grown, but if she's willing, I'd like to get to know her. I'd like her to meet her brother and sister. I'm married now but that shouldn't make a difference. I'm willing to take the good with the bad — tricks and all."

Sitting across from Donald on the couch, Big Momma felt a sense of relief for the first time in a long time. "So how is Latoya doing? We haven't heard from her in many years. She just up and walked away, left her child behind. Mimi been struggling with what her momma did for years. It's a shame when a child can get used to living with a piece of a momma, but lose her mind when that small piece up and leaves."

"Piece of a momma?" Donald asked with a look of confusion on his face.

"I might as well tell you the truth being you might be the child's daddy. I can't see her lying to you. She wouldn't breathe a word of your name to me. Oh, believe me when I say I tried everything under the sun to get her to reveal who you were."

Donald slouched down in his seat and let out a frustrated sigh.

"I'm truly sorry things worked out like they did. I'm not gonna sit and pretend it was all on Latoya. It's just that I was a child myself and when Latoya told me she was pregnant, I sorta denied the fact that it could have been mines. Now that I'm a grown man, I'm willing to accept my responsibilities."

"Well, your change is good to hear about, but did you ever consider what your first reaction did to your firstborn, leaving her out here alone in the world?" Big Momma had tears in her eyes. "It was bad enough her momma was never there for her but the least you could have been was a father. "

She paused and took a good look at Donald before going on.

"Don't think I'm putting all the blame on you. That damn daughter of mines wasn't worth shit either. She didn't even help raise the child. She up and run off every chance she got leaving her baby for a broken promise. The last time she left, she never bothered to call or send a card. Son,

I'm sorry to tell you, but your daughter is all but ruined. I did my best but the problem was that it wasn't me she wanted to do for her. You come in here talking all high and mighty, making promises about what you willing to do. You better mean every word you say 'cause you got a lot of work cut out for yourself."

Donald sat quietly for a moment. He felt anger rise as he found himself staring down at this big homely woman sitting across from him. Driving cross-country and walking to the front door to get talked down to was not what he expected. He could have stayed at home for all this.

He was trying to make a difference now. Did Big Momma understand that? Besides, it was not like Latoya was a saint.

"Big Momma, I'm sorry things happened the way they did but, like I stated before, I didn't know about Mimi. Latoya told me she was mines then told me she was not mines. It was not until a few months ago that I got a solid answer."

'Maybe I should leave,' Donald thought.

"How is Latoya?" Big Momma asked suddenly changing the subject. The frustration drained from her face replaced with a kind of hopeful excitement.

"She's fine." Donald felt himself getting uncomfortable.

He had promised Latoya he would not say anything about her new life, but he knew he was going to break that promise.

"Well," Big Momma said in a demanding tone, "tell me about my baby. I know she done found her a piece of a man. That's the only thing that could keep her away from here for so long."

"She made me promise not to mention her new life to you," Donald said quietly. The shame he felt was written across his face. He found himself stuttering and sweating all at the same time. If she asked him anything else about Latoya, he was going to tell her whatever it was she wanted — no needed — to know. He, himself, was a parent and he could not imagine being rejected by his own child.

"I don't understand her. She wanted me to pretend we didn't know each other." Donald held his head down when he spoke and kept rubbing his hands against his pants leg. "The only way I was able to get her to tell me about Mimi was to threaten to tell her husband that she had a child."

"He don't know about us?" Tears immediately filled Big Momma's eyes. Her big body slumped into the couch and she kept shaking her head back and forth.

"No. He only knows about the life Latoya made up. She's gonna have to fix her lie 'cause I intend for Mimi to visit my home."

"Well, I won't bother with it anymore. Mimi always said I need to leave it alone. Guess that's what I'm gonna have to do. Can't do much else with the truth staring me in my face." Big Momma wiped the tears from her chubby face, got up and walked out of the living room.

Donald squirmed in his seat. Running out of the house was his first thought, in order get away from all this newfound confusion that was introduced into his once neatly kept world. This was not what he had expected his life to come to: explaining to a mother that her daughter had erased her out of her life was as strange as it got for him.

"Here's some pictures of Mimi," Big Momma said coming back into the room and handing Donald some photos. "That child is so much like Latoya it's scary. How? I can't tell you 'cause her momma wasn't never around. They both live to chase dreams."

Big Momma slowly eased herself down beside him.

"Latoya, she's looking for her happiness in a man and Mimi, she's looking for her happiness in money. They both found what they was searching for and I'm willing to bet, what I got left of my miserable life, that neither one of them is nowhere near happy."

Donald sat in shock looking at the first picture of Mimi sitting in a wicker chair looking to be about nine years old smiling into the camera. If Big Momma had not told him so, he would have sworn it was his Harmony he was looking at with the same big green eyes and long wavy hair as Mimi. They both took after his father, a man his mother always talked down about.

Flipping through the other pictures Donald could not help but smile to himself. A feeling of guilty pleasure took hold of him. He felt he had cheated fate. He often found himself wondering about his children's future. What would they look like? Who would they be like? Here he sat holding a piece of the future in his hands—Harmony.

"She looks just like my baby girl, Harmony," he told Big Momma grinning.

"She looks just like Latoya to me. You say you used to live around here?"

"Yep, but once my mother took to moving, she never stayed settled for too long anywhere. I was born here—me and my brothers. My father bought property but, once he died, my mother sold it and we moved away. I moved back here and went to school for a while, then she up and moved again."

"Seems like your momma was chasing something, too."

"Never did figure that part out. She always told us, since our father died and left her plenty of money, she intended to enjoy her life and see the world. That meant we would see it with her."

"Well, that must have been nice. Me, myself, I had to work hard 'cause Latoya's father wasn't into taking care of his responsibilities. Ran off soon as I told him I was having his baby."

Donald got quiet and sat the pictures back on the table. The way Big Momma pronounced the words 'ran off' made him feel uncomfortable again.

"Don't mind me," Big Momma said noticing Donald's reaction to her statement. She pushed the pictures again toward Donald again saying, "I ain't never got over that man abandoning me and his child. Donald, you didn't know, so I can't rightly blame you anymore. But Latoya's daddy, he knew."

"I'm sorry..."

"Sorry about what? You didn't have nothing to do with that imitation of a man."

"It just don't seem right you repeating that situation in your life again."

"Never made much sense to me either, but I was raised never to question God. Can't say I never did, but I can say I didn't let anger live in my heart for too long."

"I guess that's the best way to go about it."

"Child, it's the only way to go about it. Can I fix you something to drink—lemonade or tea?"

"I'll take some tea if it wouldn't be too much trouble."

"Trouble? Didn't I ask you if you wanted something to drink?" Big Momma said walking toward the kitchen.

"I can't get over how much Mimi looks like Harmony," Donald said as Big Momma entered the room with his tea.

"I can't get past how much she looks like Latoya," she said drinking her tea.

"Harmony and Mimi take after my father, Willie Joe Johnson. I don't recall much about him, but my mother always stated he was a dark man with blue eyes."

"What's your father's name?" Big Momma asked in a whispered tone. Lord, she wanted so much to mishear what Donald had just said.

"Willie Joe..."

"Oh my Lord up in the Heavens! I don't believe I can handle all this mess!" Big Momma screamed and dropped the cup of tea she was holding.

27

Stacy Williams

Stacy got ready for work with no problems. Her mother did not have to coax her into getting up any longer. Since her father found out about her plans to attend school, he informed her she could quit her job. Even though she would not be attending classes for awhile, he insisted that she start studying beforehand.

"This is my last day of lying to fat women about looking good in drab colors," she said with a smile on her face.

She rushed out of the door without having breakfast. She felt she could not get to work quickly enough. Sitting at the bus stop, she realized she wanted this day to be over. This was the first day of her new beginning. Making her father proud was now her only mission in life. After all, he deserved it. He had sacrificed his whole life for her. All her daddy ever wanted was the best for his baby girl. Tony had gotten her off track but that part of her life was over. No, she had gotten herself off track because all Tony ever wanted was Mimi.

"Damn, I miss you, girl," Stacy said about Mimi.

Her mind went back to the night she talked bad about Latoya and called her all those names and for what—to try and impress Tony, a nigga who never liked her in the first place?

Stacy's life went downhill from that moment. She lost the loves of her life —both her father and her best friend— in a matter of months. What she shared with Tony was all in her mind and even he got tired of pretending that they had something important because it was not long before he all but told her to go to hell and leave him alone.

"Alone" was where she was left. All she had was a dead-end job and a bunch of memories, and those memories tore at her heart.

Recalling her friendship with Mimi was heartbreaking. It seemed a lifetime ago since she called her best friend up to laugh and talk about something that happened in her life. Here lately, Stacy had not had anything to laugh about. Her life seemed to be on repeat—switching between boring and painful.

At that moment, Stacy decided she needed to talk to Mimi and tell her she was sorry. All she wanted was to have a friend again. Without a second thought, she started walking to Mimi's house. What did it matter if she did not show up for her last day of work? If they called home, she decided she would lie and tell her father she went to the community college to talk to her counselor.

If she was going to lie, it would be for Mimi. Wasn't that the way it had always been? The both of them would lie and cover for each other. They had each other's backs like that, which was another reason why their friendship was so strong.

Stacy felt good about her decision until she actually arrived at Mimi's apartment door.

'What if Mimi is still mad at me? What if Mimi won't let me in? Maybe she had a new best friend and doesn't want to hang out with me anymore,' Stacy thought. *'She might not even be at home.'*

Stacy took a deep breath before knocking on the door.

"Who the hell is knocking on my door at this time of the morning?"

"Me," Stacy said under her breath.

Mimi opened the door, staring at Stacy, who was looking down at the ground at her scuffed shoes.

Finally, Stacy looked up at Mimi and asked, "Are you going to let me in?"

Mimi reared back and placed her hand on her hip.

"Why would I allow you in my home? No, let me rephrase that. Why would you want to enter the home of a whore? Not only am I a whore, but my momma was one, also."

"Mimi, I'm sorry. I was out of line talking to you like that. You are my friend, my best friend. Now, let me in so we can talk."

Mimi stood her ground, blocking the door. "Stop with the bullshit. I don't have any friends. My only friend was murdered. If you are coming around here looking for Tony, you are two days too late. You missed the party and believe me when I say we had a ball."

Stacy pushed Mimi out of the way and walked into her living room.

"Tony is the last thing on my mind. I came here looking for you. I'm tired of not having anyone important in my life. I'm tired of missing the only person I ever had. I don't need Tony. True, I thought I did, but now I know I don't. I wouldn't give a damn if you were having Tony's baby. I don't want to be his girl. I would love to be his child's godmother."

"Baby?" Mimi said slamming her door shut. "What the hell are you talking about? I ain't having Tony's or no nigga's baby."

"That's just a figure of speech," Stacy said. Stacy walked over to the love seat and sat down. "Mimi, I need you to forgive me for being an asshole."

Mimi sat down on her couch across from Stacy.

"I don't know if I can. You of all people know how I feel about my momma. Still, that didn't matter to you when it came to something you wanted, something you felt was important, something that was always mines.

"Stacy, I don't know what to think about you anymore. You made me feel like I didn't know you. I felt like I was talking to a stranger, not my friend. After hearing you that night, I feel like you were always judging me—not just with Tony, but also my lifestyle. You don't think I saw the way you looked at me the night I used you to help me out with that trick? Your eyes called me all kind of names. It just took the incident with Tony to make you speak the words that you felt. Our friendship changed the night you didn't want me to walk you home."

"You volunteered not to walk me home."

"I figured I'd do you a favor, make things a little easier for you. Us separating meant me not having to look at you judging me for what I had did."

"Mimi, that's not fair. I just didn't understand that night. I mean, it took me a minute to digest what had happened. Regardless of what you did, I didn't intend for us to stop being friends because of it."

"Stacy, you gave me the same look women used to give my momma.

Then, later, you called me the same names women used to call my momma. I could take that from anybody else but," tears came to Mimi's eyes, "it cut like a knife coming from my best friend."

Stacy swiped clumsily at the tears that suddenly stung the corners of her eyes.

"I'm sorry. I was hurt and I wanted you to hurt. I thought I was in love. I *was* in love. It's just that I was in love by myself. For that love, not only did I hurt you, but I hurt everything and everybody around me. Mimi, my father just started speaking to me the other day. I'm not supposed to be here begging you to forgive me. I'm supposed to be in some top-ranked college. Remember all the grand plans my daddy had for me? It was that same love that changed the course of my entire life. Mimi, please forgive me.

"All my life I have watched all the boys lust after you. None of them ever paid any attention to me. I, on the other hand, was always, 'just Stacy.' Boys would call after us and whenever I made the mistake and asked if they wanted me, the answer I got was always, 'Nah, the pretty one.'

"I wanted so much to be wanted. I wanted to be important, too. I was tired of being known as the 'smart girl.' I got that from my daddy—my perfect life. I needed to be sexy. I wanted to be known for something besides being intelligent so when Tony started paying a little attention to me, I lost my mind. I thought, *'he thinks I'm pretty and smart.'*

"Mimi, you been hearing how pretty you are since day one but it was different for me. Boys been grabbing at you your entire life. Tony was my first. I'm not gonna lie; I fell for that nigga like a ton of bricks. Him looking me in my eyes and touching me in all those secret places… man, I didn't know I could feel that special. It all but drove me crazy. I fucked up, Mimi. I got caught up in a feeling he created physically and one I created mentally."

"Damn, that's deep girl," Mimi said with a look of confusion on her face. "I never knew you felt that way. You? Jealous of me? I always felt you had everything. I always had to fight the jealous bug whenever you said the word 'momma' or whenever your daddy fussed about your grades. I never had a parent to fuss over me. Yea, I had Big Momma but she was always so mad at my momma, it made me angry with her. Still, I never let my personal feelings come between me and you."

"I know, but loving a man causes a different type of jealousy. When you completely love a man, you trust him entirely. Being that he is a man, you feel you have nothing to worry about. Your heart and mind let you know he's gonna take care of everything. Even if you have the means to do it, he is gonna step up to the plate and handle life for the both of you. Well, at least that's how my daddy loved my momma."

Stacy got quiet and hugged herself, thinking back to what she thought she shared with Tony. "Now I can see why Latoya up and went looking for that feeling."

Mimi looked away and then slowly admitted, "I don't care for love. All love ever did was break my heart."

"Me," Stacy said, "I *love* love. Next time it's gonna have to love me back, though."

"Stacy, I don't know about trusting you to be my friend again. I mean, what if some man brings this love that you are searching for into your life. I didn't have to worry about that with Sweets. She had already experienced the love of her life."

Stacy's face frowned up when she heard the name Sweets. "Mimi, you aren't listening to me. I said the next time I find love, he gotta love me back. That means me and all that's in my life. He has to accept my momma, my daddy, and you. I think ol' Tony taught me a thing or two," Stacy said laughing.

"I would hope so 'cause girl you lost your damn mind and the dick wasn't even all that."

"Shut up," Stacy said. "So, are we a couple again?"

Mimi playfully rolled her eyes then smiled big saying, "Yep, I guess so. Plus, I'm tired of lying to Big Momma about you. She thinks we stopped talking 'cause you didn't agree with my lifestyle."

"You told her that lie?"

"Yes, I couldn't tell her the truth that we fell out because of some nigga. She wouldn't understand that, especially since I ain't into loving

140

one particular man. I thought it would be easier for me to lie about our situation."

"Is she mad at me?"

"Nope, she don't blame you one bit. You know Big Momma hate what I'm doing; it's just that I'm all she has so she has no choice but to accept me. If she had another granddaughter, I'm pretty sure she wouldn't allow me to even come to her house."

"You sound like a fool. Big Momma would never stop dealing with you, Mimi."

"I don't know about all that. She poured so many dreams into me and wanted me to do all that my momma didn't. But I ain't never been able to live nobody else's life. I've always had to live my own. I don't see how people live to make another person happy. I'm still trying to figure out what pleases me."

"Mimi, you'll find it."

"I don't know about that. The only time I ever been truly happy was lying in bed next to my momma. The smell of her skin perfumed or not, was intoxicating. It actually gave me a natural high — nothing like the buzz you get from a drink or a blunt. And the feel of her warm body lying next to mine was exhilarating. Not even Big Momma's body leaves me with such a feeling of belonging. Ain't a man in the world that could top that. Folks find love in all kinds of places. My love was with my momma and she ain't coming back no more. Love for me is dead."

"You don't know that. Your momma might pop up anytime. That's just how she is. It's how she has always been."

"She ain't coming. I won't say I'm okay with it but I will say I've learned to accept it. Big Momma always talking about how God loves the world and how he gave his only son. I won't argue with Him about caring for everybody because He did give me Big Momma. I could have been left out here alone. But I do wonder if He loves us all the same. I wonder how he chooses who gets a momma and who don't. When I was younger I used to think God was mad at me."

"Mad" Stacey asked?

"Yea, why else would He take what I loved? But the older I got I figured He was just complicated and something's weren't meant for folks to understand. That's when I finally left it all alone and gave *myself* a peace of mind."

28

Latoya (Walker) Wills

atoya walked quietly into the bedroom. She had been fighting with
herself about how to do this. Her father —or whatever it was that
came to her— was right. It was time for an honest change in her
life. No matter how hard she tried to fight the change, she knew it had
to be done.

Him coming to her made her face what she had been putting off her
entire life—accepting who she was and what she came from. Maybe she
did not come from top-class people but Big Momma was a good person.
Big Momma spent her entire life caring and looking after her the best way
she knew how. Big Momma had raised her own daughter after she ran off
and left. So what Big Momma was not the preacher's wife, but she was
a hardworking individual who worked two jobs to provide for her child.
Big Momma even proved she was willing to spend the rest of her life in
jail by pulling a pistol in church to try and kill the man who had brought
harm to her baby girl.

Latoya had spent her life trying to run from herself.

No matter where she went, it always came down to the same thing—
nothing. Not a thing was gained from her faking it. No matter how many
men she lied to, no matter how many church functions she attended, it did
not change the fact that she had a baby girl back home, a baby girl who
worshiped the ground she walked on. She also had a mother who needed
her, a mother who, long ago, learned to accept all of Latoya's faults and
shortcomings. Big Momma did not even yell at her for not being there to
raise her own child when she walked through the door.

Latoya spent a lifetime searching for perfection and it was already in
her life. Mimi was as perfect as it got. Mimi was supposed to be upset
with Latoya for leaving her, for not spending every holiday with her, for

not giving her the attention a child was entitled to have. Mimi was not even upset. Instead, she would grab Latoya and hug her every chance she got. Not once did Mimi ask why she was not around or why they never opened a single Christmas present together.

It was settled.

"Anthony, we need to talk," Latoya said sitting on the edge of their bed. Latoya's voice was all but a whisper and her head was held low.

She had to do it.

"What's on your mind baby? You been acting kind of strange lately," he said, taking off his reading glasses and setting down his Bible.

"You don't know me." Tears swelled in Latoya's eyes.

"What are you talking about?" Anthony said sitting up on the bed.

"I'm sorry I had to put you through this. It's just that my life has been so damn complicated. I been trying to make up for some mistakes I made in the past. Maybe if I hadn't been raped as a child, I wouldn't be at this point in my life. If only I had of had a normal childhood, I would not have allowed all those boys to touch me and have their way with me. I been looking for a peace of mind for a long time. I thought you were the peace I was searching for. I thought you were my prize for having to put up with so much wickedness."

Latoya looked up at Anthony. She wanted so much for him to grab her and hug her, to tell her everything would be all right. Would he love her the way her father said he would? Would he be willing to move Heaven and Earth to remain in her world? She got nothing but a puzzled look from her husband, so she kept talking.

"I'm sorry you were made to be part of my healing process, but baby, I'm not the person you think I am. Whatever you do, please don't think any of this was intentional. I would never have hurt you on purpose."

"Hold on, baby. What are you saying to me?" Anthony said in disbelief.

"I'm saying it's time for me to go. I can't pretend any longer. I'm tired." Latoya let out a long breath. "I'm tired of living in this made-up world. You can't begin to know how hard it is for me to continue pretending, pretending to be someone and something that I'm not. Every day of my life is an act with you."

"No!" Anthony yelled and reached for Latoya hands. The tone of his voice said he would work things out with her. His actions were saying he was willing to continue being her husband, no matter what.

"No," Anthony said. "You don't understand. I love you and all this nonsense you talk about rape and boys having you, that doesn't matter. A child being raped isn't her fault. Letting boys having their way with you, as a child, isn't your fault. I mean your parents were old, so they couldn't give you the attention you needed.

"We can bring all these demons to my father. He will pray for you. My mother can counsel you. Baby, you don't have to leave. We can work this..."

"Stop!" Latoya yelled, interrupting Anthony and snatching her hands away from him. She wanted so much for their problem to be that simple. But what she had revealed was only the tip of the iceberg. All his Christian talk of prayer and change was not going to fix the mess Latoya had gotten herself into. Prayer would not be able to erase Mimi nor Big Momma from her world.

"That's what I'm talking about. You don't know me. My parents aren't dead. I never knew my father. He didn't claim me a day in my life. My mother is alive. She's raising my daughter; a daughter who is now meeting her father, Donald Johnson, the new member of our church, for the first time.

"What do you think your father would say to those truths? Do you think he is willing to pray for those demons? What about your mother? Is she still willing to have me at the dinner table anymore? Are these ungodly hands acceptable to be held during prayer meetings anymore? Baby, you don't know me. I am the very thing your family looks down on and I can't play the game anymore. I need to go and see about my child. She loves me for the real me." Latoya was in tears.

Anthony jumped over the bed and slapped Latoya across the room. "Stop lying to me you stupid bitch. Why are you lying to me? You don't have a daughter. Your parents are dead."

Anthony wasn't willing to accept Latoya's truths.

"I'm sorry, Anthony, but I'm not lying," Latoya said, clutching her jaw, which stung from her husband's slap. "I'm tired of lying."

"Your parents are dead. You don't have a child. There is no way you slimed your way into my family." Anthony jumped on the floor and started choking Latoya. "I'll kill you before I let you embarrass me like this."

"Please, Anthony," Latoya said in between breaths. "Please, I'm sorry. Don't kill me. Please, I…. can't breathe."

"You don't deserve to breathe, you lying bitch." Latoya's deception had turned Anthony into a person she did not know. She saw fury enter his eyes, and had no idea the thoughts that were racing through her husband's mind.

She did not know that Anthony was debating life and death at that moment. She could not hear him questioning himself about how it would be easier for him to tell his family that he snapped and killed her than to reveal what she had just revealed to him. She could not hear him trying to reason the madness that he had just heard to his father, who was the same preacher who would ask pregnant, unwed teenagers to stop attending Bible class, who used their family in sermons as examples of how families should be.

She was among the dutiful wives who sat on the front row every Sunday with their heads held a little higher than the rest of the congregation, obedient to God or face the wrath of punishment if things fell out of order.

Having the congregation questioning their family was not something that could happen, and Latoya knew that. She knew that her husband was raised believing that order was the only way of life and, now, she had put things out of order.

Suddenly, her husband jumped off of her. The evil that overcame his face changed to embarrassment.

Latoya coughed, gasping at the air and followed her husband's eyes to their doorway.

There stood Little Man.

Anthony jumped up, grabbed his keys and ran out of the house.

Latoya caught her breath, grabbed her purse with one hand and grabbed her baby with the other.

'Momma, I'm coming home,' she thought, and began the journey to the bus station.

29

Willie Joe Johnson

Willie lay in his cheap pine box tired, but with a new sense of relief. It was not a relief that gave him the feeling that all his troubles were over because he knew his maker had not decided where to place him eternally or else he would not still be in the cheap casket his wife placed him in many years ago. Nevertheless, it was a relief that took a bit of the worrying off his once distraught mind. Willie noticed his once constantly overheated body had cooled down a bit. He was not the cool he wanted to be, but he most certainly was not the hot he had grown accustomed to being. He did not understand why he was allowed to enter the world one more time and give his daughter a piece of advice.

He wanted so much to embrace his daughter and tell her how much he regretted not getting to know her when he was given the chance. Instead, he had to scream and fuss about what she needed to do, something he did not have the courage to do with his own wife. No matter what he wanted to do, fate was chosen for Willie. His mind was at ease and that was enough for him. Sure, he opened a can of worms that both his children, Latoya and Donald, needed to sort through but if it meant saving his granddaughter, well, they would have to deal with it.

Them being brother and sister was not nearly bad as Mimi trying to find her way.

'Oh, I ain't gonna make like them being brother and sister is a good thing. Matter fact, it's terrible. That's probably the reason I'm still in this box and haven't landed in my afterlife. But see, I didn't have no control over that. Well, it's more like I didn't know nothing about it. My maker didn't permit me to see all that took place in the lives of those who are part of me. What I did see, I did my best to change. Ain't Latoya headed back home? I didn't even intend for Donald to be part of Mimi's life, but I'm glad he is.

MIMI

One fact I do believe I done discovered about Mimi is the fact that she takes life for what it is. The child ain't never had no real momma. All she ever had was a piece of Latoya and that was more than good enough for her. Mimi had to grow up with truth on her plate. She wasn't one of those children who was allowed to believe in the Easter Bunny or the Tooth Fairy. Her young world was full of facts, with no room for fiction. And, regardless of being left and fending for herself, she always wanted her momma, Latoya.

Mimi learned to carry her momma's love in a steel can 'cause the clear purse hurt too much. She refused to let people see what she dreamed about, wasn't gonna allow the world to laugh at what she wanted but couldn't have. She knew what folks thought about her momma and knew they would roll their eyes and make fun of her for wanting something that didn't want her back. She knew what her momma was and she loved her anyway. Now, do you really think her momma bedding with a man who happened to be her brother is gonna take any of Mimi's love away from her?

I don't think so, either.'

30

Mimi Walker

The look on Mimi face said she was not happy about the meeting Big Momma had arranged. It was a meeting she thought she wanted her whole life but, now that the day had come, she was not sure she was prepared for it. Her first thought was that it would only add confusion to her defined world. Maybe she was not living right but everything was in order; well, in a type of order she could tolerate. Her life was simple. All week long she watched as her money piled up from letting older men have their way with her. Vile as it seemed, sex with strangers was as easy as putting on a pair of jeans. All she had to do was pretend and lie—pretend she liked them stretching and pulling her body into all types of positions and lie about enjoying it. Sometimes, it got even easier than that; a few of the old freaks were just lonely and needed somebody to listen to them. As crazy as it sounded, those were the tricks who paid the most.

Come Sunday, Mimi would either call Stacy up to hang out and off to Big Momma's house they went. If Stacy was busy with schoolwork, Tony was always willing to stop his fatherly duties and drop in and spend some quality time with her. Stacy knew Tony and Mimi were still seeing each other, but she never said a word about the relationship. Everything was cool until Big Momma had to call with some important "information," as she described it, messing up the order that Mimi had carefully structured.

Mimi headed for her front door, and then sat back down on the couch. She did not know if she needed a daddy. She never had one before, never even wanted one. Sweets did mention the fact that her strength must have come from him, and that was the "good enough" reason to meet the running-off nigga. Mimi did figure out that, had he stayed around, Latoya would have never went running off looking for a "good man." The one time she asked Latoya about her real daddy, Latoya told her to forget him and like a trained puppy and she did.

Daddies did not seem important to Mimi. Latoya was always promising to find her a "good one" but Mimi soon came to realize that was more for Latoya's comfort than hers. She could remember it like it was yesterday: Latoya lying in the bed next to her describing a nice man she had met who would soon marry her and take them away from all of Big Momma's yelling and fussing. Mimi would look as if she was happy about the situation but, in reality, all she wanted was to leave with her momma. Mimi did not know why they needed a man to make this long-awaited move.

Latoya never found that "good man," so the move she was always dreaming about never took place.

A lifetime later, and the call finally came with Big Momma excited to tell Mimi that she needed to get over to her house around five o'clock so she can meet her father.

"I got a trick at five o'clock," Mimi's replied unconcerned.

Big Momma all but lost her mind at her response. After she promised to pull her gun out of the attic and send her to meet her maker, Mimi decided it would be best if she went on over at the designated time.

Walking through the door, Mimi wondered how long the meeting would take. She called and informed Henry, her good-paying trick, that she would be running about an hour late. She wore a pair of tight leather pants, a leopard half-shirt that revealed her toned stomach and plentiful cleavage. Big, gold, hoop earrings hung to her shoulders; a pair of six-inch leopard printed "fuck me" heels donned her feet and all of her long silky mane was pulled into a single ponytail on the top of her head to give her the 'little girl play grown-up' look that Henry was crazy about. Her makeup was on point, deep red lipstick covered her full lips, ruby-red blush coated her cheekbones and a dark blue eyeliner encircled the outer region of her big green eyes. To finish it off, Mimi wore heavy blue eye shadow, making herself resemble one of those dancers from the eighties. She figured, if she was meeting her father, he might as well get to know the real Mimi. Besides, if she did not hide her profession from Big Momma, why should she play the good girl role for him?

"Girl, why you ain't got on no clothes?" Big Momma asked, snatching Mimi through the door and into her bedroom, which was off of the living room, before Donald could get a glance at her.

"Big Momma, please," Mimi said waving her hand in the air in an uncaring manner. "I had a date planned. You demanded me to come so, I came. I really don't have time for all this mess anyway. What's the big deal about this nigga coming into my life now? Am I supposed to be grateful? I'm grown. There ain't nothing he can do for me. Unless he knows somebody that would like to buy what I'm selling, I ain't got no use for him."

Before she knew it, Big Momma slapped her across the face. "No, you don't," Big Momma said, grabbing Mimi's arm and pulling her down on the bed. "I'll be damned if you think you gonna run outta here. Your father has driven a long way to meet you. Him and his wife and your brother and sister all came on a count of you. You wanna blame everybody in the world for what yo' momma did to you. I have allowed it this far, but not today, child."

"What has my momma got to do with this?" Mimi yelled, rubbing the handprint Big Momma left on her face.

"I can come back later," Donald's voice came through the door.

"No, you can't. Have a seat and we will be right with you. Just give us a minute. She'll be out in a second."

"He can leave!" Mimi yelled.

"Child, don't make me slap you again," Big Momma said through clenched teeth. "That boy knew nothing about you. He just found out about you a few months ago. Came here soon as your momma told him she had his child. He was willing to risk his family for you. How you think his wife feel about you? Well, it don't really matter 'cause either she has to accept you or move on. I refuse to let you treat him like a stranger off the streets, though."

The look in Mimi's eyes told Big Momma she was not alone anymore. And all these new feelings that came with being a daddy's girl only added more confusion to Mimi's once put-together world.

Big Momma sat on the side of Mimi and whispered in her ear, "I'm sorry, baby. I hate putting my hands on you. Just please give him a chance."

Mimi held her head down and new tears began to flow from her eyes. These tears cleared up a lot of confusion in Mimi's once misunderstood world. All the anger she once felt about all men except Tony started to slowly slip away. Slowly, she took the rubber band off her hair and let her hair fall to her shoulders. Without thinking about her actions, her hands went to the wet napkins sitting on Big Momma's nightstand and she began to wipe her face.

"You mean to tell me, the man sitting in the living room loves me? But he don't even know me, Big Momma. How he gonna love a stranger?" Mimi continued taking off her heavy makeup. "What if he finds out what I been doing with my life? You think he gonna be mad at me and leave?"

"He don't care about all that mess. All he wants is to meet you. All this selling yourself is just a phase you been going through. You can change."

Big Momma dug in her closet and pulled out a pair of jeans and a T-shirt Mimi left over before moving out with Sweets. "Put this on and put on a pair of my house shoes. Ain't no way in hell you gonna walk out of my room wearing those damn shoes."

"Change," Mimi said with fear in her voice. "Big Momma, I don't know if I can be anything else. Who I am now is all I know to be. I been so mad at men, I don't even know if I can love him the way he loves me."

"You gonna have to love him unconditionally, the same way he is willing to love you. Mad at men," Big Momma said with a light laughter in her voice. "How you gonna be mad at men in your line of work?"

"Big Momma, it's all about taking their money. I overcharge them and hate them all while I'm doing what I do. Don't blame me 'cause I ain't never ran across a decent one in my lifetime. Half the men at church come to purchase my services."

"Lord, I ain't trying to hear all that mess."

"Well, it's the truth," Mimi said, slipping on the clothes Big Momma lay out.

"Maybe, but that don't change the fact that you gotta get past all that and learn to love your father like a daughter is supposed to."

"How do I go about that?"

"I don't rightly know. I never had the opportunity to meet mines. You got a chance that me or yo' momma never had."

"How am I supposed to love a stranger?"

Big Momma stood on the side of Mimi looking confused for a moment. The thought of him being strange to Mimi never entered her mind. It was not like she had many proper men folk in her life. All she had to compare him to were the filth that paid to lie next to her.

"Well, child," Big Momma said in slow drawn out tone, "that he is, but if you walk on in there and introduce yourself he won't be a stranger anymore, now will he? You won't be an only child anymore. And being that I'm getting on up there in age, when my time comes and the good Lord calls me home, I won't have to worry about you being left out here in this big ol' world alone."

The look in Big Momma's eyes told Mimi this meeting was more for Big Momma than herself. Big Momma always worried too much. She worried about her health, worried about Latoya, and her last and biggest worry was Mimi. No matter how much Mimi tried to explain to Big Momma that she could take care of herself, Big Momma refused to listen. She started to remind her that she was a big girl and could handle whatever the world threw her way. She had managed since she walked out of Big Momma's house. Not once did she come crawling to her asking her for a place to stay or money to pay a bill. The pleading look on Big Momma's face told her not to say a word.

"Okay, I'll give him a chance."

Mimi slowly walked into the living room. The feeling in her stomach was not something she was used to. A new nervousness was catching hold of her body. This was completely new to her. She was used to being in control of her emotions. Not even turning her first trick made her this nervous. Maybe it was because up until this moment, everything was predictable.

All her life, she knew what was going to take place. Big Momma was going to give her whatever she asked for, Latoya was going to pop in whenever she felt like it, and Stacy was going to be her best friend. It was all as simple as that. Loving those three people was easy as pie. The few changes that did occur, she learned to adjust to. Sure, Latoya not coming home was a huge shock to her system but, after she got over the pain, she managed to put herself back in motion. Even losing Stacy for a period of time did not hurt as badly. Besides, Sweets made up for all the bad that entered her world.

Now, in the blink of an eye, Big Momma wanted her to love this man because he was her father. "Father" was the only reason that was given to her.

Fathers are supposed to be there a child's entire life and not pop up one day expecting an immediate spot in a child's world. Stacy's daddy was a father. He was there from day one, pushing and instructing her on how to live. Whenever he came home from long hours driving the truck, he went over her schoolwork with her, praising her for all the good work she turned in. Mr. Williams took her to the park and bought her ice cream cones. Even when he was tired, he forced himself to take her to the zoo and swimming.

The man sitting in the living room with his picture-perfect family never shared a single day of my childhood with me,' Mimi thought.

Loving a father, or any other male figure, was not something Mimi envisioned in her future. Maybe loving the money he provided, but loving who handed her the money did not add up to her.

"Hello," Donald said standing as Mimi entered the room. He rushed and hugged Mimi.

"Hi," Mimi said shyly and instinctively hugging him back. The sound of her voice scared her. She did not expect to be so kind to him. The feeling of his arms wrapped around her caught her off guard. His hug did not feel like the hugs she encountered when the other men hugged her, but was warm and safe, not wanting and perverted. Donald's hug brought back memories of a period in her life when all was promising and safe —at least that was what she assumed because of her momma's promises.

Usually, Mimi did not talk about Latoya to anyone but Stacy. The mention of Latoya's name brought on a string of questions that reminded Mimi of how different she truly was.

"Where is your momma?"

"Why is it that you don't live with her?"

"How old is she?"

"Is she sick?"

Grown folks always wanted answers to things her childish mind could not answer. But the day Latoya told her she was taking her away with her, Mimi walked into school with her head held high and told everybody. She felt she had the proof she needed to show them that her momma loved her. Latoya not taking her only made her feel shame. Mimi never wanted to show her face at school again. The sickness turned to sadness and helped her stay home for a short while. After the sadness, anger seeped in and there it stayed—until he hugged her.

"This, here, is your brother, Donald Jr. and this little girl, who looks to be the spitting image of you, is your sister, Harmony."

"Oh my God, she does look just like my Harmony," the lady standing next to him said excitedly before grabbing Mimi and embracing her with the same love-felt hug Donald had just given her.

"This is my wife, Loretta, your step-momma."

"Hello," Mimi said trying to shake Loretta's hand.

"Hello. I don't think so," Loretta pushed Mimi's hand out of midair and embraced her once more. "I'm going to be your stepmother. Shaking hands isn't appropriate. I take my hugs plentiful and warm, if you don't mind."

Knowing no other way to reply, Mimi smiled. "Sorry," she whispered.

"You don't have to be sorry. Sit yourself down." Loretta motioned Mimi to have a seat next to her and the children. Harmony instantly jumped into Mimi's lap. "Harmony, this is your sister, Mimi," Loretta said with a beam in her eyes.

Mimi looked down at the girl and immediately fell in love. The self-reflection of Harmony brought back memories of innocence to Mimi, a period in her life she had long forgotten about. Harmony's radiance of light opened up places she tried to forget existed, places of laughter, purity, and compassion. Mimi had learned to accept the space she carved out for herself in the world. She had actually convinced herself that happiness did not belong to her. Happiness, she thought, was something God granted to good people, special people, and people more deserving instead of people whose mothers walked off and left them alone in the world. Most certainly not people who allowed boys and strange men to touch them in sacred places that were meant to be touched by a true lover.

"She does look a lot like me," Mimi managed to say. "

'So, this is how honest true love feels,' she thought. *'These people I don't even know are willing to accept me.'*

"Well, I'll be," Loretta said looking between Harmony and Mimi again. "I did all the work having the babies and they resemble everybody but me."

"There's a reason for everything," Big Momma said in a factual tone. Donald shot Big Momma a sharp look. She turned slowly and walked out of the room.

"What is she talking about?" Loretta asked.

"We'll discuss it later."

"Donald," Loretta said trying to mask her sudden alarm. "I don't think I can handle too many more surprises."

Big Momma's slow dragging steps interrupted the stillness of the room. "We might as well get it all out in the open." Big Momma laid a worn black and white photo on the coffee table. "Loretta, if you willing to forgive him for a daughter he didn't know about, you may as well forgive him for a sister he had no knowledge of."

"What is she talking about Donald?" Loretta had a look of confusion on her face.

"I'm talking about the picture of that man on the table."

Donald jumped up from his chair and grabbed the picture of his father. He was young when his father died and his mother did not have any pictures of him.

'This is him,' Donald thought holding the only piece of what should have been the most important man in his life. Willie did not look anything like Donald or any of his brothers. He was a tall dark man, with handsome features.

He looked just like Latoya, Mimi and Harmony.

"Donald, what is going on?" Loretta asked, wanting some answers. Donald continued staring at the photo. He was at a complete loss of words.

"Oh, child," Big Momma said with pain in her voice.

"This is the first time I seen him, outside of his obituary picture," Donald said quietly. He was still focusing on the worn out picture. He no longer sounded like a grown man but like a child. He found himself in his daughter's place—a lost child. He, too, was just now discovering a piece of his history. "She never talked about him and refused to allow us to visit his people. I know he had people. Everybody got people. And just one of us children mentioning his name brought out the devil in her."

"You can't keep holding on to the past. You gotta let it go," Big Momma said patting Donald on the back. "Sometimes us older folks make mistakes, too. Whatever yo' momma did, she did 'cause it was taught to her. Don't look at the situation as her purposely harming you. Tradition has a lot to do with the nonsense we tend to repeat. I'm not speaking just to hear myself talk. I speak from experience."

Big Momma took a long drawn out breath and continued speaking, except instead of looking at Donald, she was now eyeing Mimi. "I ran my own child off 'cause of something my grandma passed down to me. My grandma fussed, whooped and hollered about me bringing Latoya into this world immorally. I knew how bad it felt to be called such names by the only person who cared for me. And what did I do? Turn around and did the same to my own flesh and blood. Made it so she couldn't stay around and raise her own child. Was I purposefully trying to run my baby away from me? No! But by the time I realized what I was doing, she was long gone. No mother would ever intentionally hurt her own babe."

"But she did," Donald said laying the photo own the table. "Not only did she ruin things for me, but now my child has been affected."

"How?" Mimi said only understanding the part of the conversation that dealt with her and Latoya.

The room held an uncomfortable silence for a moment. Big Momma closed her eyes, looked to the Lord and began talking. "Mimi, all that I'm about to inform you is not your fault. How you take it is up to you. You might get upset, but just know one thing. Know you ain't no freak. Know you're loved and always will be. Remember that children make mistakes and that's what your parents were when you were conceived—children, who got caught up in grown folks' mess."

Mimi had a nervous look on her face. Out of nowhere, her hands started sweating and her heartbeat quickened. She was scared, scared of not knowing and not having the simple control of her surroundings she once had before agreeing to attend this "meeting."

"What Big Momma? Please save the speech. Tell me what the hell is going on!" she yelled and jumped out of her seat.

"Your father and mother are sister and brother."

"What?" Mimi screamed. "What kind of sick shit is this?"

"Oh my God," Loretta uttered.

All the comfort and safeness Mimi felt only minutes earlier disappeared. That warm belonging place she had momentarily allowed her body to sink into spit her out. The space did not want her. The space recognized her as a fraud and fake. She saw images of people laughing at her, calling her a fool for believing that she could be normal. The smell of her impurity must have seeped out of her pores and alerted the guards of virtue to kick her out of the safe place she was bold enough to enter. Maybe it was the strong corrupt smell of all the tricks she had so easily let crawl in between her legs that gave her away?

The little, shy, bewildered girl was once again the street smart, know-it-all hooker who did not allow silly things like feelings get in the way. She learned long ago to kick emotions to the side.

'Calm down,' she thought. 'Show no emotions; caring is for the weak.'

Mimi looked at Harmony with a sad smile, sent her back to her parents and quickly headed toward the front door. She heard voices call her name, but continued walking.

Opening the door, she got the surprise of her life. There, in living color, stood Latoya holding a black, nappy-headed baby boy. She reached to hug Mimi, but Mimi did the unspeakable. She pushed her mother to the side, almost knocking her and the baby down and continued walking down the street.

If she hurried, she could make her date with Henry. Mimi found herself craving this once-despised old man. Their dates usually consisted of him lying on the side of her, running his mouth with an overly large head, potbelly and baseball legs. He liked to brag about all the money he made and complain about how ungrateful his sorry-ass wife was. Before the meeting, it would have been the usual quickie. She would have tolerated his drawn out conversation and hurried him back to his pathetic wife. Not tonight, tonight Henry was going to fuck her long and hard, even if she had to rape him. She needed him to set things straight for her, help put her life back into her defined order.

PART 5

31

Donald Johnson

Donald sat in the dingy hotel room staring at the red light blinking on the phone. He knew it was Loretta calling him wanting to degrade him about the ordeal at Big Momma's house. Home was not where he wanted to be. He just did not feel like he belonged anywhere anymore. One minute he was making plans to pick up a piece of his life he left behind and, the next minute, he was watching that piece run out of his life. He needed time and space to sort through his thoughts, needed his next move to involve no penalties. He yearned for simplicity because all he had just witnessed was entirely too complicated.

After taking a personal leave from his job, he went home, packed a few of his belongings and walked out the door. Driving down the freeway, he pulled his car into the first hotel he spotted. The first couple of days he cried like a baby; cried for his newfound child, cried for his wife, but, most of all, he cried for himself. After weeping himself dry, he realized that nothing had changed.

No matter how hard Donald tried to erase everything that had taken place in his life, he could not get the look of Mimi's face out of his head. First, she was street and hard acting. Big Momma had tried to sneak her in the house without Donald noticing her in her "work clothes."

He had seen it all—the skintight leopard pants and the half-shirt, the hair pulled in a ponytail, and the globs of makeup piled on her face. However, walking out of the room Mimi had a different look, the look of a child; the child he did not get a chance to witness grow up.

Not only was her appearance different, but her face revealed a fresh look, a look that was not completely inviting, but illustrated that she was willing to give him a chance. Mimi appeared to be wanting the change she thought he was about to bring. The harsh voice he heard screaming behind the door vanished. The sexy stroll he noticed enter the house departed.

All that altered the moment she found out the news about them all being inter-related. She looked at them like they were some type of sick freaks and silently hurried out of the dwelling but not before turning back into the hardened prostitute she was when she first entered the house.

"What kind of bullshit did I start?" Donald quietly asked himself.

The phone rang shortly, taking Donald's mind off Mimi.

Loretta,' he thought. How she had found him, he did not know.

He had no answers to the questions she asked so what was the purpose of him answering her calls.

"I didn't know," was the only reply he gave to the hundreds of questions that flew out of her angry mouth on the ride home. Good thing Harmony and Donald Jr. were too young to understand the mess that their father had created. They sat quietly as Loretta called him all kinds of names. One minute she was crying to herself and the next she was wailing like she was at her mother's funeral. In between all the crying, she would scream at him, accusing him of purposely ruining her life. "Why didn't you just leave me home? Why did you trick me into marrying you? I had no intentions of being part of your sick life."

How could he begin to explain what he did not understand himself? Loretta knew the situation with Donald and his father and how his father died when Donald was a child. Half-listening to her rant and rave left space for Donald not to reply about the whole ugly ordeal at Big Momma's house. It only made sense for him to drop what was left of his family and drive away.

He knew the next step was a divorce. He would not even ask Loretta to continue being his wife after all of this. "I should have told her the whole truth before taking her to meet Mimi," Donald said out loud. "Hell, it was hard enough convincing Loretta to accept her."

Before Loretta put him out, Donald decided to take it upon himself to leave. The one time he did answer the phone, she started in on him, yelling and screaming. He quickly hung the phone up and sat there in a daze. Besides leaving his wife, he did not know his next step. He knew he would have to leave town. There was no way he would be able to live in the same town with Loretta and not have her. He would put in for a transfer at his job and go somewhere no one knew him. "A fresh start," Donald said before drifting off into the nightmare of Mimi's speechless deranged expression.

32

Latoya (Walker) Wills

Latoya laid in her old bed feeling out of place. It just did not seem right without Mimi pulling and tugging at her covers. No, she was not a child anymore, but that had never stopped her, in the past, from crawling in the bed with her momma and claiming her space. That was the silly reunion Latoya thought would take place. She and her baby would pick up right where they left off. Only this time there would be more joy to the equation because Little Man was now part of the family. Only things did not go as Latoya planned. Her once dutiful daughter had transformed into a woman, a woman who hated her momma.

Mimi was finally lashing out at Latoya and she did not know how to deal with the rejection. Not once since she had started running off and leaving her child did Mimi ever reject her. She was the reason Latoya ever came home. Time had changed a lot of things since her last departure. Mimi had grown tired of being Latoya's baby fool. She was not even putting up with Big Momma. The girl had her own apartment without the help of a man. She up and did what her momma could never seemed to accomplish—became independent.

Big Momma stood looking at Latoya and Little Man as they lay in the bed feeling a mixture of emotions—disturbed and relieved. She was disturbed about the way Mimi had ran out of the house. The child was so upset she did not even speak to her momma as she stomped away. She pushed Latoya to the side like she was a stranger. All the yelling Latoya was doing calling Mimi, and the child never even turned to acknowledge her momma was talking. She just marched on up the road. The look in Latoya's eyes told the whole room how she was feeling—defeated. She walked past Donald and his family without speaking and went up to her old room. Donald excused himself and headed toward his van. His wife and children followed with Loretta looking at her husband as if he had plenty more explaining to do.

Still, with all the commotion that was caused by the family secret being exposed, Big Momma was more than overjoyed to have her child home and, this time, she did not come alone. Though the boy was a year-and-half-old, he was brand-new to Big Momma. That man of hers must have been something special in order for Latoya to agree to have the child because Big Momma knew Latoya had already had a number of abortions. Mimi was truly lucky to slip through.

I got my baby back,' Big Momma thought as she watched Latoya cradle Little Man the way she used to cradle Latoya.

True, Big Momma had learned to live with the fact that she may never see her daughter again. Still, the pain had not left her heart nor did the ache of giving love that would not be returned. With all of Mimi's preaching about Latoya being where she wanted to be and even Donald stepping in and informing her that Latoya was hiding from her, the want of her only born had lingered in her heart. The only thing that changed about her feelings was that she did not speak them out loud. She learned to keep her desire in a closed place, a place only God was allowed to enter because she never stopped praying.

"I'm sorry, Momma," Latoya said without even turning to face her mother. "I done caused so much trouble. Wish I would have just left things as they were but..."

Latoya thought of telling Big Momma about her dreams and Willie Johnson coming to her on the porch, then decided against it.

"Seems I haven't ever been good for nothing but ruining stuff. Wish I could leave, but I'm tired of doing that, plus I ain't got nowhere to go. I messed up things with his daddy," Latoya looked toward Little Man who was now fast asleep, "and turned everything upside down soon as I walked out of our door."

"You ain't going nowhere," Big Momma said as she walked toward Latoya and squeezed a space on the bed for her to sit. "You right where you belong, at home. This here is yo' house. When I pass on over to the other life, all I have goes to you. I didn't work two jobs so the city could end up with what's rightfully yours. So settle in, baby girl."

"What about Mimi? I came back here for her and she don't even want me no more. This pain I got is worse than any I have ever felt before. It's worse than when Pete Stone promised me he'd marry me. That nigga took me all the way to Washington with the intentions of me becoming his whore. I packed my things and headed back home, only to wait for the next man to sell me a bridge. I learned to live with men walking out on me. But I don't know how to live without my baby loving me..." Latoya stopped before finishing her sentence. "I'm so sorry, Momma."

"It's all right, child. We can't change what's been done. It's all water under the bridge. What's important is the fact that you came home. That's all yo' momma gives a damn about. You need to know yo' child ain't running from you. She's running 'cause she's confused like you used to be. The only difference is, you didn't know what you was running from. Mimi, on the other hand, is running from the truth. When Donald first came here, we found out that you two were brother and sister."

"What!" Latoya sat up and almost knocked Little Man on the floor.

"You heard what I said. You and Donald share the same father, Willie Joe Johnson. All this was made clear when he told me his daughter looked just like the man."

"Momma, no," Latoya moaned.

"It's true. Ain't nothing we can do about that. It's done and over, in the past. What we need to focus on is Mimi. The news upset her real bad. She won't take my calls or answer the door when I go by. I figure I'll give her a little time before I try to push myself on her again."

"My half-brother, Momma? This is a bit much for me to handle. I no longer know what to say to her myself. How can I explain that to my child?"

"You can't. How does she expect you to give her the answer to a question you know nothing about? It's a shock to us all. That's what we have to make her understand."

Big Momma lifted her heavy frame off of the bed and walked toward the door.

"We just have to give her some time."

33

Mimi Walker

Mimi's work ethic had increased tenfold since her encounter at Big Momma's house. In order to stop her mind from thinking too much about what had taken place, she decided to put her all into her work. For the first time since she started seeing Tony again, she had no time for him. Stacy was not even given the occasional Sunday lunch they used to share.

She decided against taking Sundays off.

Working was important for her sanity. Too much free time meant she had more think time. Thinking meant trying to figure out why she and her parents were inter-related? Were they really related? Was her momma that out of place? Did Big Momma really not know who her daddy was?

And Big Momma, with her good churchgoing ass. How did she allow this to happen? She always played the role like she knew everything. Turns out, she did not know shit.

'Thinks she can run my life but can't even tell her own daughter not to fuck her brother,' Mimi thought.

Then there was this person Donald. What was he about? Looking all pitiful, pretending he wanted Mimi in his life.

'Sorry to inform you, mister, but I'm all of a grown woman now.'

"You missed out on my life," Mimi said.

Did they really expect her to accept all this bullshit?

All the questions were slowly driving Mimi crazy. If she sat too long, they danced in her head nonstop. She imagined herself being a little girl and grown folks looking at her like she was a freak. Old whispers turned into loud laughter. Teachers' inquisitive looks became knowing stares. Children's chuckles were no longer harmless teasing.

'They all had to know,' Mimi reasoned.

The thoughts Mimi were having scared her. She found herself pleading with tricks; she needed them to stay the entire night with her. The quietness in her apartment was terrifying. It was during those quiet times that these thoughts overtook her. She did not want to think

With no one to trust, Mimi held her feelings inside. She considered telling Stacy, but then quickly changed her mind. Once before she allowed Stacy to know her true feelings about life and Stacy went and used those thoughts against her.

Sure, when she came back she promised to never do it again, but the hurt of Stacy's words never completely left Mimi.

All behind a no-good nigga.

No, Mimi could never totally trust Stacy again. If she ever got mad at Mimi and used her past to hurt her, Mimi would not be able to handle it. Sure she had allowed Stacy back in her circle, but only with limits. No more shared deep conversations, trusting secrets, or talking of her feelings concerning her momma. Their relationship consisted of now; all past dealings were tucked away. If Mimi was going to allow Stacy access to her friendship, that meant she and Mimi were one-on-one. Their friendship would never again include conversations about her momma, grandma, and certainly not the father whom she just met. It all boiled down to Mimi needing a companion and, since Sweets was gone, not many people were standing in line for the job.

Her next optional release was Tony. With him being married, Mimi did not feel the close connection anymore. Yea, he still had the schoolboy charm to him. Sure, he was just as fun and always willing to creep away from his fatherly duties to please Mimi, but it was not the same. Tony was a different person. The responsibilities of him being a father got in the way of their playtime. Instead of laying with her until she decided it was time to go, he rushed out of the house barely kissing her goodbye. He did not even have the decency to turn his phone off on his visits. More than once, after getting off the phone with his wife, he hurried off claiming some family emergency.

Even her tricks gave her more attention than he did. Still, with all the changes, Mimi refused to charge him. A few weeks after being married,

Tony approached the topic of him giving her money for their dates.

"You couldn't afford it," Mimi replied, but his question truly hurt her feelings.

Didn't he know they were better than that? Most times, they had sex without using a condom. He was the only person who was allowed to enter her completely. Didn't he realize the importance of that act? She was willing to totally share herself with him. Tony asking to pay her put him in a light Mimi had never thought of him as—a trick. The question affirmed the fact that he also thought of her as just a whore and not a friend. Evening knowing this truth, she refused to stop seeing him.

The only alternative was to pretend the meeting did not take place. After analyzing the whole ordeal, it did not make sense to stress over what did not fit into her organized world. Before she walked into Big Momma's house, her life had no problems. The couple of times Big Momma strolled to Mimi's door knocking, begging to come in and talk, Mimi refused to answer. What could she possibly say to fix things? And her bringing up the fact that Latoya was home did not make things any better.

What was Latoya here for anyway?

Mimi chopped Latoya's visit up as a way to drop off the little boy she had in her arms. That had to be the reason for her coming. Didn't she realize Big Momma was too old to be raising another child? The poor boy was going to end up in a home because Mimi had no intentions of being a mother to no child, not even to a brother she did not know.

'No, Latoya hadn't learned anything', Mimi thought. *'She's still the same selfish person she has always been. He'll end up just like me—a throwaway child. No, he'll be worse,'* Mimi reasoned, *'because he won't have Big Momma.'*

"Left your door unlocked again," Tony's voice broke into Mimi's bedroom.

'Damn, I'm really tripping,' Mimi thought. Even though she needed somebody to talk to, Tony was not who she had in mind. She had half of a thought to tell him her prices.

'Isn't that what he really wants to know?' Mimi stared at Tony, her eyes expressing the fact that she really was not feeling him.

"You hear me talking to you?" Tony said before sitting on the bed.

"Did you lock it?"

"Yea." Tony spread himself across the bed and started rubbing Mimi's back.

She jerked her body away.

"Sorry. Didn't mean to upset you. If you want me to leave, I can do that. Just say the word." Tony sat up on the bed.

"Have I ever been one to hold my tongue?" True, she was upset with him, but seeing him made her change her mind about him leaving.

"No, but actions speak louder than words."

Mimi turned and faced the wall. She was not sure how to respond to his comment but she knew it was going to be as honest as the words that came out of Stacy's mouth the night she had caught the two of them together. "It's just that I ain't in the mood for a rush job. I get those all the time from my tricks. They treat me like a whore and I expect that kind of treatment from them. You rushing in and out of here, now that's gonna take some getting used to. Seem like you starting to see me in the same light."

"Mimi, it's no secret I'm married. You can't expect me to come here and stay all day. I don't tell my wife my whereabouts when I leave the house. True, we don't have the time we used to have, but my feelings for you haven't changed. Not long ago, it wasn't me who was rushing out the door. If I recall correctly, all I got were Sundays. No matter how I felt about the situation, I knew I had no control over it. I dealt with it. You think your feelings are less than mines when it comes to being hurt? You think it didn't sting when I was made to walk out of the door before I felt my time was up?"

"Tony, that's not fair." Mimi wanted to yell, but she did not. How she controlled the heat that rose to scorch her words, she would never understand. But she brought her voice back down and said, "I always had a little time for you after we had sex. I never got up and left right after we were done."

She continued looking at the wall. She was ashamed of needing him, ashamed of doing what she told Stacy she would never do—plead for a man's attention. True, he was married and already in a relationship. Still, love was not the title she was ready to give the emotions she expressed.

Mimi decided to bank on respect. She was demanding her respect from Tony. She could hear his movements. First, he stood up, and then he sat back down. His breaths were long, symbolizing that he was taking in her remarks. Confusion and being careful not to hurt her feelings was what Mimi gathered from his actions. That was a good sign because a trick would not give a damn what came out of his mouth. A trick's only purpose was his own pleasure.

"The rules are different for us. You have complete control of your life. I have to answer to somebody," he said. "My freedom is gone, Mimi. I have a wife. Maybe she isn't the one I envisioned myself with, but she's the one I have."

That was not the reply Mimi wanted to hear. Tony was slowly turning the table, making her realize that if she had lived a different life, she would have been his wife. She did not have time to argue with his truth. His conversation was making her head hurt, making her think too hard. Hadn't Big Momma done enough of that lately?

"So, how much time you got?" Mimi turned to face Tony. Her voice was no longer heavy and filled with hostility but indicated that she needed what little time he was willing to share. The reality of the fact was that she needed a friend, and he was the only one up for the job.

"About two hours."

"I think I can make two hours work."

A smile slid across Tony's face. "Baby, I'm sorry about the way things are."

Mimi put her finger up to Tony's lips signaling him not to talk. "We won't journey down that road any longer. Besides, we only have a few minutes to enjoy each other. Anyways, it's not you. It's me. I started feeling like you thought of me as a whore. I mean, I know I am, but not to Big Momma, not to Stacy and, I hope, not to you. In Big Momma's eyes, I'm a granddaughter. Stacy sees me as a friend.

"I don't know what position I hold in your mind. I knew before you were married. Now, you are starting to blend in with the rest. But, like you said, I know your situation. Listening to you, I guess I have to accept things the way they are or lose you. Before you came here tonight, I thought I was willing to let you go, but looking into your eyes makes me see things differently."

This was not the speech she saw herself giving Tony. She was supposed to tell him to get out, and let him know he was not needed in her life. She had enough problems with niggas to be putting up with his soft ass. He fell into the category with the rest of them—a married man crawling around town, paying for pussy.

Right there was where her thoughts stopped. He had never purchased sex from her. He offered, but she insisted that their relationship was too sacred. Without her realizing it, Mimi put meaning into the time shared between them. Now, he was a part of her defined world, a part of what was normal to her. Kicking him out would only add more confusion to what Big Momma had already confused. Tony had to stay. How else would she fill up her lonely moments? What she did realize was the fact that she needed Tony—not just for sex, but also as a friend. She was accustomed to having him around. Mimi knew she needed to accept all as it was.

No more surprises or new people were going to be a part of her life.

After listening to Mimi's speech, Tony picked up the phone and called his wife. He calmly explained to her that he would be later than he originally stated. Four or five hours was the guesstamation he figured it would take him to fix the friend's car. The mysterious friend needed some serious motor work.

Tony hung up the phone, turned to Mimi, and said, "I have never thought of you a whore. Your profession is what you do, not who you are."

34

Latoya (Walker) Wills

atoya quietly looked through the meat at the *Save-More* grocery store. It had taken her a month to venture out of her mother's house. The thought of judgmental stares kept her close to home. Outside of sitting on the porch watching Little Man play in the front yard, Latoya never left the house. Big Momma forced her out of the house that day. She insisted that Latoya go to the store and purchase their meal. Tired of fussing with Big Momma about hiding from life, she grabbed the money and headed out of the door.

Leaving the house gave Latoya the quietness she had been craving. True, her mother did not complain about the things she used to complain about. Now, all her complaints were centered around Mimi. Day in and day out Big Momma pleaded with Latoya to go to Mimi's apartment and talk to her.

"Go and give that child an explanation. You need to make her understand none of this is your fault. It's your responsibility, Latoya. It's part of being a mother. There are some things I can't do and this is one of them." Big Momma would go on for hours about the importance of Mimi knowing the truth.

Latoya had no idea what to tell her. It was not as if she had planned all the mishaps Mimi was facing. Everything she had done in the past was for a reason, a reason that she thought would lead to bettering her life. A better life for her meant a better one for her daughter, everything from going to bed with Donald, to jumping up leaving to searching for a man to take to care of them, to getting married. At that point, in her confused life, each step was a better one. Every time she made a choice it was to make an improvement in her life. Nothing she ever did was meant to harm anyone, especially not her baby girl. Her intentions were to give

174

better than her momma gave. Each stupid childish decision actually made good sense in her eyes since the time she made them.

That was the problem—she was a child making grownup choices.

Maybe the first time she ran, it was to get away from Big Momma and all the fussing about her having a baby. Between Mimi crying and Big Momma screaming, Latoya could not take it. It was not until she was on the road meeting men who would take care of her and who would actually take her in that she came up with the plan to get married and come back for her baby girl.

At first, all the men loved her. They loved her in different ways. They would show her the world, give her anything she looked at.

What she liked most about the men was the way they touched her. Their touches were nothing like Joe Parker or Donald's. These men put Latoya in a comfort zone that was totally new to her. Joe was rough and forceful; his eyes were beady scary. The whole ordeal left her with thoughts of blood, pain and tears. Even though he managed to maintain a steady calm voice, it did not match his movements. A peaceful sweet tone slowly came out of his mouth but his hands tore at her clothing. He even had the nerve to wipe the tears out of her eyes as he forced his way into her stiff body.

Donald, on the other hand, reminded Latoya of rejection. The first rejection came in the form of him ignoring her at school, though it was not so bad. She could handle it as long as he continued making his visits. When they were alone, Donald was warm and caring. He took his time when they made love, kissing and caressing her, touching her in places she never knew could make her feel good. He made it a habit of looking her in the eyes when they made love. He said he needed to see the pleasure that they shared.

Yea, she knew about his dizzy-ass girlfriend, but if he really belonged to somebody else, what was he doing in her bed? Latoya soon learned the truth about his relationship with Loretta when Latoya got pregnant. Even though things were good with Donald, he turned out to be like all of the other men she met. He left her, too. Every time she mentioned having a daughter back home with her momma, they slowly slipped away from her.

None wanted the extra baggage of a child.

It was not until she slowed her pace and stopped dating the street type that she bumped into Anthony, whom she thought would be different. With him, she took things slow. She decided not to mention Mimi and just let it ride as she tried to feel him out. Before she knew it, she was in love, but nothing like the loves she had before. He was a real gentleman and was not even interested in sleeping with on her at first sight.

Anthony was not taken by looks; her colored eyes or her long wavy hair did not seem impress him. He was interested in what she thought about.

"What you thinking?" was his favorite question. He wanted to get to know her.

Latoya could not just give him a simple answer. He wanted details.

"Why you thinking that?" He wanted a reason for any answer she gave.

Anthony was the type to dig deep. He put some clarification in her confused world. They would spend hours talking on the phone or riding around in his car. Through their conversations, Latoya learned who Anthony was and what he demanded out of her if he decided to have her as his wife. Of course, she did give it up to him before they were married. But that did not change things between them. In fact, their sex added a layer of intimacy to their relationship that she had never experienced before. Their bond was solid. It was after them sharing themselves that he made crystal-clear what he wanted. It was not much; all he wanted was a decent God-fearing woman.

Latoya decided she could be that. She could change in order to be a part of his world. Still, there was the question of whether she should tell him about Mimi. All the other times she mentioned her daughter, the men left. She could not bear the thought of Anthony leaving. He was what she had been searching for her entire life—a good man who was willing to love her and not take advantage of her. Yea, she had told Mimi she would find her a good daddy, return and give her the family she herself never had. But maybe that was not God's plan. Why would God send her somebody as special as Anthony only to have him leave? No, God would not do such a cruel thing.

God must have wanted Mimi to stay with Big Momma. "Nothing was planned," Latoya whispered to herself as she pulled her attention from her thoughts and back to her grocery run for big Momma. She looked around at the pig's feet really not knowing how to choose a good cut. After inspecting the pink meat, she decided on the package with the least amount of hair. Pig's feet were not her favorite meal. Latoya knew she would not be eating them, so she decided on chicken for her and Little Man. She walked over to the chicken, unsure if she wanted a whole chicken or legs. Little Man loved legs, but she, herself, was a thigh person. Mimi used to be crazy about legs, too. She especially loved legs that had been stewed in Big Momma's dumplings.

The thought of Mimi running out of the house jumped into her head.

'I didn't know things would end up like they did. I was simply a woman in love,' Latoya thought. *'Momma went through the same thing with me. I'm sure when she allowed Joe in her house, she didn't know he would end up in my bed. I don't blame her, so why Mimi gotta blame me? Why is it that I accepted what wasn't planned, but she gotta be so crazy about the situation? I didn't know Donald was my brother no more than Momma knew Joe Parker was plotting on having his way with me.'*

Latoya picked up a whole chicken and threw it in her cart.

"Chicken tonight?"

Latoya looked up and saw a tall, browned-skin, handsome, clean cut man with a sparkling set of white teeth man smiling at her.

"Maybe," Latoya said moving on. The last thing she needed was a man. Men seemed to be a constant problem in her life.

"I didn't mean to scare you off," he said following her. "It's just that I've never seen you around here before and..."

Latoya stopped abruptly. Waiving a dismissive hand at him she said, "Look, I ain't got time to be standing around talking to strangers. I got a mother and kids I need to get home and feed."

"Kids?"

"Yea, two of them." Latoya answered.

"You don't look to have two children."

"You calling me a lie?" She said shooting him a crazy look.

"No, I didn't mean it like that," he said shaking his head. He smiled before adding, "It's just that my ex-wife has one baby and she would pay to look like you."

Latoya couldn't help but smile at his last comment, but she quickly erased it.

'No,' she told herself. 'Not again. I don't have time for this nonsense. Yea, he looks good, but they always do.'

Latoya walked away.

"Hey, why you acting so mean? We haven't even introduced ourselves. My name is Davis Goodman." He held out his hand, indicating that he wanted to shake hers.

"Mines is Latoya," she said dryly. Latoya looked at his hand at if it were a trap, a trap she was not falling for.

Davis quickly put his hand away. "Don't think I done ever come across a bear as mean as you," he said chuckling.

"What would you be doing messing around with bears?" Latoya held the same mean look in her voice as she wore on her face.

"Used to hunt 'em in Alaska," he said looking her in the eyes.

"Oh, well, it ain't hunting season."

"I wouldn't be expecting to find no bear in the grocery store. Wasn't expecting to bump into something as beautiful as you, neither. You ain't from around here."

"Yes and no." Why she changed her tone with him she did not understand. "I was born and raised here, but I left after my first baby was born. She grown now."

"Well, y'all must look like sisters."

Latoya laughed at his remark. She was actually flattered. Before this stranger, it had been years since anybody called her beautiful or gave a compliment without reason.

Anthony used to say nice things about her in the beginning of their relationship, but that all changed about a month into their marriage. His remarks came only before and during sex. And Mrs. Wills only gave commands. With all the instructions she gave her remarks were more like she was teaching a dog, such as, "That's much better" or "Now, you are getting it."

Nothing Mrs. Wills said ever seemed sincere. Latoya was constantly made to feel as if she was in some type of training. No matter how much she improved, the tests never seemed to stop coming.

Latoya could honestly say that she did not miss being around all that nagging. She quickly wondered how Anthony had explained her absence to his know-it-all mother, but dismissed going down that line of thinking when she focused back on Mr. Davis Goodman's face.

"Well, we aren't sisters." Latoya's voice was light and less threatening.

"How long are you in town 'cause, I don't mean to sound so forward, but I would really like to take you out."

"Out?" Latoya questioned skeptically. The last thing she wanted was to run into some of the women from town. She was not ready for that. "I don't know about all that."

"Oh, I'm sorry. I didn't know you had a man. Well, I see you ain't got no ring on your finger. If he knows like I know, he'd better place one there real soon."

Davis turned to walk away.

"I ain't got no man!" Latoya heard herself yell after him.

He turned around with a wide smile on his face and walked back up to her. "Look, I'm gonna give you my number." He went in his wallet and pulled out a pen and piece of paper. "Call me when you figure things out. I'll be looking forward to it."

Latoya stood dumbfounded as he handed her the number and walked off. She stood in the checkout line feeling guilty. She knew she should be more concerned about Mimi, but Davis' inviting smile kept dancing around in her head. Even though she knew there was a big possibility that he could be a wolf in sheep's clothing, just the chance that he might be the one made her feel a little jittery.

He came across as a nice man, even after she mentioned she had two children. He did not run off even though she practically told him to get the hell away from her.

'I guess I'm guilty of being a woman. All we want is somebody to love us. Who can blame me for that?'

"Mimi!" someone called out.

Latoya turned around and saw her daughter's friend, Stacy, standing in the line next to her.

"Oh, Ms. Latoya, I didn't know you were in town," Stacy said dryly. She switched check-out lanes and gave Latoya a warm hug inspire of her less-than-friendly greeting.

"How long you been here? My goodness! You don't look like you've aged a day since I was a little girl. You look like your own daughter. Mimi didn't tell me you were here."

Latoya's hopes were dashed again.

"Well, I ain't been seeing much of Mimi. She's pretty upset with me." Latoya stepped out of line and Stacy followed.

"You must be kidding. Mimi don't get mad at you." Stacy had a baffled look on her face.

"Well, she done learned how. It's been over a month and she hasn't come back to Big Momma's house."

"A month?" Stacy was at a loss for words. True, she had not been seeing Mimi much with school and all, but she was just over to her apartment the other day and Mimi did not mention anything about Latoya being in town.

"Has she talked to you about any of it?" Latoya was desperate to find out any information about her daughter. And with Mimi not opening the door for Big Momma, Stacy was Latoya's last hope for answers.

"She didn't even tell me you were in town."

"I'll be here for awhile. Me and my baby boy."

"Baby?" Stacy looked shocked.

Latoya decided she needed to find a way to get to Mimi, even if it meant telling her little friend all of her business.

"Let's pay for these groceries and walk outside. There's a whole lot you need to know."

35

Donald Johnson

Loretta beat on the door of the hotel room with all the strength she could muster. No matter what force she placed on the door, it would not open. She tried to kick the door, but that did not work either.

"To hell with this bullshit!" she yelled as she continued banging and kicking. "You are not getting off this easy, Donald. You will not hide from the mess you have caused. You may have fooled me. Yea, you tricked me into believing you were somebody worth having in my life. Dragged me all the way from home to live in your make-believe world of happiness. But you gonna bring your ass out of this room and face the music. I will not allow you to do this to that baby. I'm not going to allow you to do this to my children. All this stems from *yo'* nasty-ass, but you can't run from nothing. God did not allow you to just be a tramp then forget about all the problems you caused.

"You should have left me at home." Loretta's voice started to crack. She was doing what she promised herself she would not do—cry.

"You should have left me where I was. But no, you had to come get me, make me believe you was gonna give me a good life. All you gave me was two babies and a headache. Made me a step-momma before I was a wife and you think I'm gonna allow you to hide from it? If I gotta deal with you as a husband, you sho' in the hell gonna deal with her as your daughter slash niece, or whatever the hell you and that woman done created."

Donald did not respond to the madness outside his door. "Donald, you hear me? Open up this door or all hell is gonna break loose!"

"Excuse me madam, but if you don't leave here at once, I'm going to call the police and have them remove you," The manager of the hotel stood next to Loretta pleading for her to go.

"Call the police!" Loretta yelled, stepping close to the manager. "Call the army if you need to, but I ain't leaving here without that no-good husband of mines."

"It's all right, Tom," Donald said holding the door open. He looked worn out. His facial expression revealed that the last thing he wanted was a mad woman shut up in a confined space with him. What he wanted was Loretta to leave. She could even shout a few more curse words at him then storm off. But once he heard her kicking at the door, he knew that simple wish was not going to come true. It even crossed his mind to let the police haul her off, but then who would look after the children?

Without much of a choice, Donald opened the door.

"Are you sure?" Tom was eyeing Loretta, seriously questioning Donald's decision. His dark-red complexion expressed the anger that he harbored at the strange woman making demands at his hotel.

"Did he stutter?" Loretta pushed Donald in the room and slammed the door in Tom's face.

"Where are the children?" Donald asked.

"What difference does that make to you? Besides, I'm the one who should be asking all the questions. When do you plan on coming home? When you going back to work? And what do you intend to do about your daughter? You can't just up and decide to act like none of this happened. You the one who thought it was all good to go and get her. You the one who needed to find your missing link. You think just 'cause she ain't what you thought she would be, you can up and decide to forget about her? No, mister. It don't work like that.

"And what about us, me and the children? You think I'm gonna allow your sorry ass the freedom that you stole from me. Oh, hell nah! You gotta fix this. I don't know how you intend on making it all right, but what I do know is that you got some figuring out to do. And it ain't gonna take place in this room. I done already called your supervisor and he expects you back on the job bright and early tomorrow morning. Transfer my ass. He was all excited about the fact that we decided not to move away.

"You think I'm gonna allow you to leave me? If you wanna go that bad, have at it. But you better believe you taking both of those rug rats you tricked me into birthing 'cause I refuse to do it alone. You think I'm gonna chase you down for some child support that ain't gonna be enough to raise two dogs properly, let alone two children? You must really think I'm that same silly-ass girl you had in high school, No Mr. Fuck Up. You take the kids and let *me* send the checks every month."

Donald quietly packed what few belongings he had and headed out the door to the office. He settled his bill, apologized again to Tom then made his way to his car. Loretta followed close behind in hers.

What could he say to anything she threw at him? It was all the truth put in a harsh way, but still the truth. Besides, he had grown tired of sleeping in the little dingy room he was renting. He missed his home, his children, but most of all, he missed Loretta.

He did not know returning was an option. He just assumed she had written him off. After all, he had written himself off.

Donald did not believe the words existed that could get him back in his home. Listening to Loretta, he soon found out it was not words that placed him back under his roof, it was his situation. He refused to allow them to be living under arrangements. If they were going to go at it for the sake of the children, it would not last. Their relationship had to be built on love, the love that he felt in his heart for his wife.

They entered their house silently. Donald dropped his bags by the door and sat on the couch. He wiped his hands across his face, sat back, looked at his wife, who was sitting next to him and said, "None of it was planned. I took you from your home expecting to give you nothing but a good life. The transfer was simply a cop out. The last thing in the world I thought you wanted was me coming back home. I know you probably don't believe it, but the only thing I wanted *was* to come home. I just didn't think you'd have me. And the situation with me and Mimi, it was all new to me." He slowly turned to Loretta, "The last thing in the world I wanted to do is to hurt you. When I came back home to get you back then, it was only to do right by you. If I had of known all this mess was gonna take place, I would have left you. Baby, I just didn't know."

"I know," Loretta sighed.

"So, if I'm gonna stay around, it's gotta be the same. We can't be living like we mad at each other. We have to be a couple, a married couple."

"Donald, I need some time."

"I'll give you some time but, if the love is gone, it will be time wasted."

"Donald, I hope the love isn't gone. Lord knows I hope it isn't. We done put a lot in this. We have a lot to lose."

"Recalling what you said to me at that hotel, I'm starting to think it's lost."

"I'm not allowed to express my anger?" Loretta's voice was no longer soft. "How do you think I feel Donald? What was I supposed to say? I tried calling. You refused my calls. I went through a lot of emotional channels alone. I had all these questions and you were nowhere around to answer them. In the middle of my confusion, I was forced to take care of the children, alone. It took everything in me not to drop my babies off at the police station and drive out of town."

Loretta calmed down at her confession.

"I actually put them in the car with intentions of doing just that, dropping them off at the station and driving away. I thought, *'he created this mess, he can deal with it.'*

"As I approached the station, the thought of what I was about to do scared some sense back into me. Then I called you at work and your supervisor tells me you put in for a transfer. Donald, you tell me what you wanted to hear?"

Donald sat quietly. He was once again in that place he hated. Years ago, when he came to take her back, his plan was to give her a happily-ever-after life. The reality seemed to be, though, that he only brought her pain.

"All I'm saying is allow me to vent. Don't ignore me. Let me say the things I need to say out of anger. Could you at least give me that? Don't pick up and run off. You brought me here. I didn't come on my own. And you are right about us being together. I don't think I could stand it if we continued to stay together for the sake of the children.

"Donald, I haven't fallen out of love with you, but I am upset with the current situation. It was bad enough I had to accept an outside child, yet, I was willing to face the fact it happened before our marriage. True, we were together, but I allowed you to be a different person then. I've come to realize all this new stuff, though it affects me, is your baggage. Baby, you cannot run from it. Our situation can be fixed with time, but it's gonna take some sweat to make things right with that poor child who ran out of that door. I couldn't believe nobody went after her."

36

Mimi Walker

Mimi sat in the dinner lounge at a trendy restaurant in town. Tony was almost an hour late, but his tardiness did not dampen her spirits. She was overly excited about the fact that he was actually taking her out—a real date and with Tony at that. They had not been out since high school.

It felt good to be out in the public with a man and not sneaking around with another woman's husband. Technically, Tony belonged to someone else, but in her heart of hearts, he was hers. Tonight she intended to play house and not whore. Mimi had not had a lot of practice being a lady but, somehow, Tony always pulled the innocence out of her. In his presence, the tough girl faded away.

Tony made her understand why women loved men. Over time, he put reasoning behind Stacy's actions that night Stacy caught him and Mimi together. Mimi did not even know when she came to love him. All she knew was the fact that he added stability and consistency in her life. He was the only one who absolutely and unwaveringly cared about her. The wife thing was something she had to pretend did not exist, which was not hard because pretending was a big part of her job requirements. As long as he continued to show up when he did and be the friend that he was, she would always return the friendship.

Besides, things on the home front were a little rocky. It seemed someone had informed his wife about the time he and Mimi were spending together. The wife could not take it, so she up and moved back to her mother's house in California.

Tony said the fact that he was seeing a whore, as she called Mimi, made her blow her top. It wasn't so much that it was a whore. It was the fact it was me, Mimi, the town whore. She knew damn well about my past with Tony. I guess she thought because she

186

got pregnant, and that they got married, I would be out of the picture.

'Yea, he begged her back, even told me we would have to stop seeing each other. What did I do? I turned into the weak woman I've always despised. I cried and begged and yelled for him not to stop seeing me. Later, I called him and apologized for my actions. Told him he was married and needed to conduct himself as a married man, and that he didn't want his daughter to turn out like me.'

Later his wife came back, but that did not stop anything between Mimi and Tony. She caught him leaving Mimi's house late one night, and she left his house for good that time.

'So here I sit, waiting for him to treat me to a night on the town. I cancelled all my dates, not only for the night, but for the entire weekend.'

Mimi could not believe she and Tony would be sitting out in the public for everybody to see. She tried talking him out of it; she told him she would cook a nice dinner at her place or, if he just wanted some fancy food, he could pick it up and they could go to a nice hotel room. And not the kind of rooms that Mimi frequented on her dates, but the kind people had to make reservations in order to get.

She even offered to pay.

"No," he demanded and insisted that they spend a night on the town.

He said he did not care that people might think he was buying pussy. He would not be looking around wondering if somebody is watching him. He did not care that a member of his church might be having dinner with their family and see him sitting at the table with a known whore. Tony said he wanted to take Mimi out.

"Hey baby, sorry I'm late. I had a phone call hold me up." Tony sat at the table with a look of concern on his face.

"We don't have to stay," Mimi managed to stay. She did not mean a word that came out of her mouth. There was nothing more she wanted than to spend a night on the town with the only person she truly trusted.

"Oh no, we not going anywhere. It's…nothing. Now is not the time nor the place. I don't intend to bring my problems to our dinner."

"Baby, I'm not going to enjoy myself if I know something is bothering you. What is going on?"

"Lisa called."

Mimi's face went blank at the mention of Lisa's name. She liked to refer to her as "the wife." Not mentioning her name made her less of a person and less threatening. "The wife" put her in a category with the rest of the women Mimi found herself up against. But there was a difference between Lisa and the other women: Lisa was a threat. She had papers and the heart of the man Mimi loved, a man she did not even know she loved until Lisa came into the picture.

Up until Lisa, Tony was a guaranteed fixture in Mimi's life, even though she treated his desperate affection like a childhood crush. Up until Lisa, Tony was just a familiar fling with no attachments. Up until Lisa, Tony was the male friend she had wrapped around her finger. Even her best friend did not possess the power to pull him away.

Lisa was different.

When Lisa hurt, Tony hurt. Even now, he had a look on his face that revealed he was in pain. Lisa put a twist into Mimi's relationship with Tony. Mimi could tell when Tony was having problems with her. When he came to her bed, he brought Lisa's problems with him. Sure, he come around after she worked him over, and put her magic touch on his body, but their relationship was not what it used to be now that Lisa was in the picture.

"And," Mimi managed to say.

"She wants me to move to California with her and the baby or she will be filing for a divorce. Said that's the only way our relationship will work." Tony was quiet for a moment then he whispered, "I don't want to lose my child."

"What did you say to that?" Mimi knew she had no right venturing into his personal life. After all, he was still a married man. He still legally belonged to Lisa.

"I told her I don't know."

"You're lying." Mimi's said sharply.

Dinner was not going to go as planned. "Tony, don't you know after all these years I can tell when you are lying to me?"

"Baby, please. This is not the time nor place." Tony lowered his voice hoping Mimi would follow his lead.

"Tony, I don't need you to start lying to me. I need you to tell me the truth."

"I told her I would come, but I had to. She was crying and I just needed to get off the phone and get to you."

Mimi noticed the couple next to them turn toward their table and she lowered her voice.

"Tony, our reservations were at seven o' clock. Baby, you were in no hurry, you came extremely late. I'm not as stupid as you must think. There is no way you could have hurried off the phone to make it here to me and still be this late."

Mimi gathered herself before getting up from the table. She expected him to chase her and beg her to come back to the table. Instead, he watched her walk off. Before exiting the restaurant, she noticed Latoya sitting at a table with a handsome man. The man must have made a comment about Mimi because she heard her mother say, "That's my oldest child."

37

Latoya (Walker) Wills

I t came to her again.

"Latoya, you headed in the right direction, but looks to me you 'bout to turn down the wrong road. I know you think she don't need you, but the child is cryin' out for her momma's affection."

Latoya could hear the voice, but she could not see his face.

It was the voice of man that came to her as her father—the man who fathered both her and Donald. Latoya had made up her mind to hate this man. This was the man who left without letting it be known that he had fathered other children; the one who was her daughter's grandfather through both Donald and her. She wanted to run and get away from this mad person but she was in a dark place— a place so dark it was impossible for her to see her hand when she moved it across her face.

"Leave me alone. I hate you. You messed up my entire life. You the reason. It's because I listened to you I'm in the mess I am now. You convinced me to leave my husband. 'Tell him the truth,' you insisted. 'He might love you even more for that.'

"Well, he didn't. He tried to kill me. Now, I'm in a place where I gotta start all over. What I came back for don't even want me no more. My baby girl hates me. She used to love me. Used to be, I come to town and she would treat me like a queen. Didn't matter that I skipped all the holidays and a few of her birthdays.

"Now, she thinks I'm some kind of a whore, sleeping with my own brother. She thinks she some kind of freak of nature. Don't even want an explanation for how it happened. I can't half blame her 'cause I don't understand how it took place my damn self. If you think I'm gonna allow you to help me make any more decisions, you must think I'm the fool my momma was when she let you in her bed. All this mess because you had to be a whore.

"You stop coming to me trying to give me advice. You didn't want to be bothered with me as a child and I don't want to be bothered with you now," Latoya said angrily.

She tried to run, but the darkness would not allow her to get very far. She would run for a moment then stop. Each time she stopped his voice seemed to be closer.

"Latoya, I told you nothing but right. You weren't happy where you were living it up. You were pretending to be happy, but you were nowhere near happy. This place you at now is a place where you can find yourself. I never said it was gonna be easy. Nothing worth having is. Latoya, you gonna have to learn to fight for what's yours. You can't keep accepting whatever life hands you. Don't be the fool I was. Be better than me. I know it don't make much sense to you, but I love you. I come to you because I've been allowed one more chance.

"I was allowed to undo one of the wrongs of my past. I could have chosen any of my mistakes and, believe me, I've made more than a few. I chose you because you the most important thing I had and I didn't even know it — you and yo' momma. Ain't much I can do for her. She did all right after I left. I don't even fault her for taking in that slime ball Joe Parker. How can I judge her for trying to love? When I had the chance at true love, I turned a blind eye. Now, you, you my biggest concern. I want to thank you for listening to me the other time I came. You didn't have to pay me no mind. You could have stayed with yo' husband. It would have been easier. Thank you for letting me be the father I didn't have the sense to be when I had the chance."

Latoya sat quietly in the dark. She wanted to continue fussing, but she knew it would not be right. She wanted to tell him to go to hell. Wanted to ask him how dare he mention her mother. Instead, she took in all he said.

"Now, I know you tired of me preaching, and I won't be coming around no more. I done used up all the time I was allowed. But I need to tell you this before I leave you. Your baby girl is in a world of hurt. It ain't all on account of you. She's going through some things she don't rightly know how to handle. Either you gonna have to step up to the plate and demand she listen to your explanation, or you might find yo'self in my position."

"What are you talking about?" Latoya panicked at his last statement. She searched around the darkness, needing to see the person who was talking.

"Don't expect her to accept you with open arms. You have to keep fighting for her love the same way I battled with you. If you give up, you gonna lose more than you can deal with."

"What are you talking about?" Latoya yelled. She woke up to Big Momma shaking her.

"Girl, you must have been having a bad dream. I heard you yelling all the way in my room. Look at you, sweating something terrible. Calm down and try to go back to bed."

"Momma, what's Mimi's number? I need to call her."

"Child, you ain't gonna be able to catch Mimi this time of night. Either she at work or she ignoring calls from this house."

"Momma, just give me the number."

"What's going on? Why you all of a sudden demanding her number?" Big Momma stood at the edge of Latoya's bed with a look of confusion on her face. "Don't let that crazy dream you had go and make an important decision for you. You half-crazy, almost seem drunk. Lay back down and get some sleep, and I'll get you the number in the morning."

"Either I'm calling her tonight or I'm not calling at all," Latoya's voice jumped at Big Momma.

If something happen to my baby, I'll never be able to face anybody in this town again,' Latoya thought.

"Momma, you gonna give me the number or not?"

Big Momma wrote the number on a piece of paper. Latoya quickly slipped on some clothes and headed out the door. She took a deep breath before entering the phone booth across the street. If Mimi was home, chances of her answering a call from the caller ID with Big Momma's number were slim to none. Latoya slowly dialed the number.

"Hello," Mimi said in a sexy tone. She must have been expecting a trick to call.

"Mimi, I know you ain't expecting to hear from me, but baby, we need to talk. I got a lot of explaining to do. I at least owe you that before you decide to cut me out of your life."

"You missed my life. I'm not that silly girl waiting for you to drop in and acknowledge me as her daughter. In case you haven't noticed, I'm a grown-ass woman. I take care of myself and pay my own bills. I ain't never been like you. I don't run from my problems. I may even be a whore, but I don't sleep with my kin."

"Mimi, it's not what you think. Can you please make some time for me? I really need to talk to you. I mean, maybe you need to talk to me. I'm here for you now. I know I did wrong by you for a long time, but I'm here now." The phone was silent for a good two minutes.

On the other end of the line, Mimi was frozen. She wanted so much to believe her mother's words. Were they not the words she had spent her entire childhood waiting to hear? Mimi looked around her room. She glanced at the reflection of herself in the full-length mirror hanging on her wall. She wanted so badly to see the reflection of the little girl who used to wait for her mother's visits.

She needed to see the little girl who used to dream of lying next to her momma in the bed. Yet, no matter how hard she looked at her reflection, all she saw was a whore. Mimi closed her eyes and tears boldly slid down her cheeks. "She's gone," Mimi whispered into the receiver.

"Mimi, please." Latoya decided to break the silence. "Just give me a few minutes of your time. I don't expect to clear everything up. Baby girl, even I don't understand all the shit that had happened. I just need you to know that I didn't plan any of what happened to you. Donald didn't plan anything either. All this information is new to us also."

"Look, Latoya." Mimi voice had hardened. The tears she shed only seconds ago disappeared. "I don't need you. I can handle whatever comes my way. If I feel I need you, I'll call. It's your turn to wait."

Mimi hung up the phone.

Latoya stood in the phone booth crying. She leaned on the glass, and let her soul pour through her eyes.

"Latoya?" Davis pulled his truck to curb. "I thought that was you, baby, get in. You don't look so well. What's going? You live around here somewhere?" Davis got out his truck and carried her to the front seat.

"She won't forgive," Latoya cried. She found herself crying in the arms of a man she barely knew. True, she had allowed him to take her to dinner, but insisted she take a cab to and from the restaurant. All during dinner, Latoya stayed reserved.

'*He don't need to know too much about me,*' she thought as she sat across the table listening to his life story.

Here it was, not even month later, and all she hid at dinner was all she could talk about as she sat in his truck pouting.

PART 6

38

Big Momma

Big Momma sat in her housecoat in the living room drinking coffee, trying to analyze what she could not figure out. With the relationship between her daughter and granddaughter, entirely too much time had passed since they had spoken to each other. True, Mimi had the right to be upset, but not forever. She needed to learn to accept the past and move on. Latoya was not the best mother she could have had, but she was the only mother God had given her. Forever is too long to hate anybody (except that snake Joe Parker). Mimi continued to ignore her mother, even after Latoya begged her for forgiveness the night she demanded Mimi's number.

Big Momma thought, *'I don't know exactly what was said, but I saw Latoya's reaction to the phone call. I stood on my porch and watched the whole thing. Latoya was so broke down, she couldn't manage to walk home. I was grateful that nice man stopped in the truck to see to it that she got home safe. True, she was only across the street, but my poor child was completely broken.'*

Lord knows the last thing she wanted was to have Big Momma help her across the road.

When Big Momma seen that Latoya and the man were headed her way, she hurried into her bedroom.

'Some pain even a momma can't make right for her own child. The situation wouldn't have done any good, with both of us standing in the living room crying. Plus, I tried to warn her. I tried to tell her to stay put, wait until the morning. Tried to tell her to clear her mind up before she spoke her heart. Mimi taught me that. True, it don't take away none of the pain, but it will help a person feel a little better after the fact.'

The phone ringing interrupted Big Momma's thoughts. Annoyed, she picked up the receiver. "Hello?"

"May I speak to Big Momma?" a woman asked, firmly.

"Speaking, and who am I speaking to?"

"Loretta Johnson, Donald's wife."

"I don't mean to be rude, but I do believe Donald is the one who should be calling here. Now, I know y'all is married and all, but the dealing he got going on here shouldn't be none of your concern."

"I don't mean to be rude either but he *is* my husband. We do intend to spend the rest of our lives together and anything that concerns him concerns me. You may not understand it, but those are the terms of our relationship."

Big Momma figured Loretta was irritated. Hell, she heard the irritation all in Loretta's voice. Not once, though, did Big Momma consider that Loretta stayed on that phone because of Mimi.

"Big Momma, I was hoping we could talk civil. I'm not calling your home to make trouble. I'm calling because I think we need to try that meeting thing again. Donald wants to do it, but he's scared. He hasn't outright said he wants to do it, but I know my husband. All he needs is a push. If I tell him you said it's okay that we come back down, he'll come. It's just that he needs a push.

"I'm figuring he needs guidance as much as Mimi. They both seem to be a little hardheaded at times. I figure if you work on your end, I can work on mines and, with enough work, anything can come together. I know you probably thinking I'm out of my mind but that poor girl has 'bout worried me to death." Loretta's voice softened as she continued, "I tried to be mad. Believe me when I say I tried to hate everybody in that house. After awhile, I got my senses back. I realized Donald's a good man. He has grown up a lot. Yea, he was something else back in his youth, but that was then. Mimi, she's part of his youth.

"The thing I realized most is the fact that Mimi is part of him. No matter how much I let that upset me, it don't change the truth. Don't misunderstand me, there was nothing more I wanted than Mimi to be a big lie. I was praying we would get to your house and see a child that didn't belong to him. I was never prepared to share my husband with a child that wasn't mine. But then I set my eyes on that girl, and I knew. I knew she was just as much as Donald's as my set of twins. Mimi looked to be more like Harmony's twin than Donald Jr. A bigger version, but sure enough, a carbon copy.

"I knew right then and there that my prayer wouldn't be answered. All I had left to be angry at was God, and I know better than that. In time, I guess I learned to live with my new truth. I also saw that baby girl hurting when she ran out of the house. So, not meaning to take up much more of your time, I simply need to know if you'll have us back down to try and clear this mess up."

"Well," Big Momma said after listening to Loretta's speech, "it's not gonna be all that easy. Lord knows I feel like I'm talking to an angel. There's nothing more I want than for y'all to come back down. It's just that..." Big Momma grew silent.

"What is it?"

"Mimi ain't never stepped foot back in this house since the day she stormed out of here all torn to pieces."

"Oh no!"

"The child won't take my calls. She won't answer the door. I thought after awhile she would come around, but nothing has changed. I don't believe I can get her over here to meet with you."

"Well, maybe we'll just have to make a visit to her."

"I'd hate for you to come all this way only to be ignored."

Loretta sat quietly on the phone trying to figure all this new information out. "Well," she finally blurted out, "you say we can come, we coming. I won't mention to Donald the part about Mimi not speaking to you since she stormed out of the house."

"You think that's a good idea? Don't you think he should know what's going on with the child before he comes all this way? Mrs. Loretta, I'm tired of secrets. You might want to tell the boy. You say he's all messed up behind it. It don't seem too sound to have him come and get his feelings hurt even more."

"Damn his feelings. I'm more concerned with that child who's been hurt her entire life. Even if she don't let him in, at least she's gonna hear his piece. I won't let him leave until he lets his side of the story be known. That's the only way I can ever respect him again. I have to know he tried.

I know it may sound silly to you, but it's hard trying to completely love a man you don't respect. As I stated earlier, I can't blame him for his past, but I can blame him if he walks away from his responsibility today. It is his responsibility to, at least, try and make her know the truth. He's a man; he'll have to get past his pain. Besides, whether he did it intentionally or not, he's part of the reason for the problem."

"Never thought of it that way before," Big Momma said, looking at the picture of Latoya hanging on the wall. "Well, when you come down, I would like it if you stayed at my house. You gonna have to stay a couple of days. I know the child ain't gonna come around in a day."

Loretta was taken aback by the offer. "Thank you, but I think it would be best if we stayed in a hotel. It would be a pretty tight squeeze with the twins and all."

"I do believe we could make it fit."

Loretta laughed and said, "I bet you could. Tell you what, we gonna stay at a hotel but I'm sure you will entertain us during the day. I'm willing to bet you can cook a mean sweet potato pie."

"You more than right about that," Big Momma said proudly.

"Well, we will be down in a few days, so let's have a feast. If you don't mind sharing your kitchen space, I'll make my famous meatloaf."

"Usually I do all the cooking in my home, but since I'm up in my years, I'll give you the honors."

Loretta could not help but laugh. "I know you ain't joking. I'll take it as a blessing, the fact that you up in yo' years."

"When you coming down?"

"I'll have to talk to Donald and give you a call back with the details. I don't know when we coming, but I know we coming. Believe me when I say we coming, and soon."

Big Momma hung up the phone feeling a lot better than when she picked it up.

That Loretta's a special kind of woman,' she thought, walking into the kitchen. Her coffee had gotten cold.

39

Mimi Walker

Just when Mimi thought her world couldn't get any more chaotic after the recent episodes, it took one more confusing turn.

"Fuck!" she yelled as she looked at the two pink lines on the stick revealing what she already knew. This was the third pregnancy test she had taken in two weeks. The thought of her carrying a child scared her to death. Mimi was terrified. She found herself doing something she had not done in years—praying and not the simple type of prayers she did when she was a little girl sitting in church with her grandmother.

Back then, Mimi would close her eyes and pretend she was following along with the Reverend's words. In truth, her mind would be on some freaky deed she had not long ago conducted. There were even times during prayer when she would lean forward to make her breasts thrust out further than they already were, and out the corner of her eye, she would watch the men watch her. They, too, were pretending to be praying.

Not tonight, Mimi had no time for playing games with God. She needed him in a bad way; she needed him to make a change in her life. Lately, Mimi found herself on bended knees, head bowed, eyes closed, desperately trying to cut a deal with the Lord. If only He would make this child growing inside her disappear. Given one more chance, Mimi would do right by the Lord, and herself.

Last Sunday, she found herself standing in the doorway of her old church, but the familiar looks of disapproval she received from the women made her turn around and walk away. Over time, it seemed the looks had grown worse. Or maybe it was her not being able to handle the disapproving stares just as her mother was not able to handle them.

Used to be, Mimi would walk in with her head held high in the air and dare any one of the women to get out of line. But not this particular

Sunday, not even Big Momma's protection at a distance was enough to shield her from the way the members of the church made her feel. It was as if their eyes penetrated through her soul.

'They smell the bastard in me,' she thought as they watched her standing at the entrance of the church. Maybe it was the loose-fitting brown dress that gave her away. The old Mimi would have never thought of stepping foot in church in something casual and brown. She actually had to purchase an outfit in order to have something proper to wear.

She stood there, straining her neck, hoping Big Momma would so happen to turn around and motion for her to come sit with her.

'Why didn't I come a little earlier so I could have caught her before she took her seat?' Mimi thought hopelessly.

With Big Momma anywhere near, the women would have smiled and gave out a bunch of fake hugs. They would have told her they were glad she was returning home and welcomed her with opened arms. The women would have known what to say in Big Momma's presence. The way Mimi was feeling, she would have been grateful to hear the lies. Everybody in church knew what Big Momma was going through. She was forever standing up, teary-eyed, and requesting prayer for her wayward granddaughter. Big Momma always sat up front and Mimi could not bring herself to pass the evil glares of the wicked women who occupied the back of the church. So she left the church and continued praying.

After taking the second test and getting the same results, Mimi figured she was not praying right. Big Momma always said one needed to take prayer seriously, and how one needed to concentrate when taking personal time with the Lord.

Maybe that was it. Maybe it was all the worrying she was doing that was blocking her prayer from God's ears.

So the previous night, Mimi relaxed. She put all her faith in what she was asking. Her conversation was short and to the point. She did not want to drag on too long and get nervous and not focus on what she needed to request.

"No worrying," she told herself before taking up time with the Lord. On bent knees, she prayed, "Dear God, I know I ain't... I mean, I haven't been living right, but I need a big favor from you. I need you to make this baby go away. I don't mean kill it or anything evil like that. I need you to give it to somebody else. Make a miracle, you know like turning water into wine or bringing the dead back to life. I know you can do things like that.

"Big Momma has been telling me my whole life that if I put my faith in you, you can make *anything* happen. I know I haven't been living right, but I feel I can change. I don't want what my momma had. I don't want a messed up life and baby. I could handle this life for myself, but I don't want to put my baby through the madness I have been through.

"If I wake up in the morning and the baby is gone, I'll change my whole way of living. I'll get a real job, move back home, be nice to Latoya, and get in touch with my father. I'll even start school again; take some night classes. Big Momma said you know every man's heart, so I know you know I'm not lying, Amen."

Mimi went to bed feeling better. For the first time in a long time, she did not stress herself about the baby, Tony, Latoya or anybody. She closed her eyes and drifted off into a peaceful sleep; the kind she had not had since she was a little girl with Latoya lying on the side of her. So when she woke up and the test results were the same, she sat on the edge of the tub and cried like a baby.

Being afraid was an emotion Mimi did not know how to deal with. Fear was something she felt other people had to deal with. What was there to fear when she controlled what happened in her life? Other people never put fear in Mimi's heart. Up until this point, it was the other way around. Mimi got a kick out of putting fear in other people, whether it was the women who feared that their husbands and boyfriends lusted after her or the husbands and boyfriends fearing they might get caught lusting after her. Up until that morning, Mimi had control over almost everything.

She stood up and looked at herself in the mirror. She needed to know what a fool looked like, because that was what she felt like. She was a damn fool for allowing herself to get pregnant by a man who, no matter how she tried to put it, was in love with another woman.

Tony was not a real problem. She could mask her feelings about him, stay away from him for awhile and put order back into her world. The baby, however, was an entirely different matter. Big Momma was too old to be dropping the child off with, and Latoya was out of the question. Latoya did not even raise her *own* child. An abortion was an option, but Mimi was not even going to tell that lie to herself. Awhile back, Mimi had seen a film on the process of abortion. After watching the documentary, she cried for weeks. All the pulling and tearing the baby went through just about drove her crazy. Sure, the baby was not supposed to feel anything, but that did not change the fact that the baby was being ripped apart. Mimi knew she was a lot of things—a whore, a liar, even a thief, but she was not a murderer. The people at church would not be able to pin that label on her chest.

Gazing in the mirror, Mimi realized for the first time what she had been running from her entire life—Latoya. She stood there looking her love/hate relationship in the face. Wasn't that the trail she was trying to avoid? Didn't she forever promise herself she would be better, stronger, even smarter than her momma? Wouldn't men always be the victim of her long wavy hair, stunning emerald eyes and well-defined body? Wasn't she supposed to wear her dark skin tone unlike any woman on the planet? Her beautiful burnt tone made men run towards her, not in the other direction. Her almond shaped eyes pulled them in. So what if it was only for a night? Mimi's saying was, "As long as his money was right."

How would a baby fit into the picture, and where would a baby fit into her life? Mimi took a deep breath and looked at herself once more. Not only did she feel she looked like her momma, but now she felt like her.

"I'm scared," Mimi whispered. "I know why, Momma. I know why you left me. You could handle the mess the world threw at you, but it was too much for you to watch your baby girl suffer because of your shit."

Mimi leaned on the mirror and cried as all of her new reality ran through her mind.

Up until a few weeks ago, she had controlled everything. But not that day, what did she have to offer a baby besides the skills of how to sell pussy? Or how to make a man feel like he was king of the world while wishing he would fall dead so she could get his wallet and go. Yea, it was cool for her, but if she had to have a baby, she damn sure did not want her baby to live the life she was forced to live, and running to find a man to take her and her child in was out of the question.

At that point, the only thing Mimi knew was that she did not have a clue. She could not have picked the next move up if it fell in her lap. The one thing she did know was that she was now acting like a person she vowed she would never become—her mother.

Mimi's fear that she would walk in her mother's footsteps was no longer a fear, it was a fact. The fear of having a child without the skills to bring it up in the world was happening to her.

Was she carrying a girl or a boy? Would her baby be fatherless and motherless like she was? Would Tony believe it was his baby? Where was Tony? Did he leave and go to California with his wife? Mimi had not seen him since the dinner. He did not bother to call and when she finally called him, he did not bother to answer.

Mimi had convinced herself she was fine with the fact they were over. He was married, after all. Did she expect him to come running to her promising that he would make things better? He would not even allow Mimi to play the game. She was what she had always been and he was what he had always been. Tony had respected Mimi as a friend, but when his marital status changed, he had to play the part. Tony had to take up the role as a husband and Mimi putting demands on him only seemed to push him away. She reacted the same way as Stacy, but with less drama. Why did she even entertain the thought of their situation becoming anything more than the two of them being friends?

It was not long after Tony rushed out of the restaurant that she noticed she had not had a period in quite some time. She was at least three weeks late.

Mimi washed her face and went into the living room to try to calm down.

"Well, if I am going to have this baby," she said aloud as if Stacy or Big Momma was sitting across from her, "I'm going do one thing my momma didn't do. I'm gonna allow the father of my child to decide whether or not he wants to be involved in the baby's life."

MIMI

Without hearing from Tony in such a long time, Mimi had no choice but to call up his mother. Yea, she hated Mimi like the rest of the women in town. She would probably curse her out over the phone, but Mimi knew one thing: bad news travels fast.

40

Donald Johnson

Loretta stepped out of the car feeling exceptionally good. The ride to Big Momma's house went well. The children did not act up and conversation between her and Donald was pleasant. Just as Loretta had told Big Momma, it was not hard to get Donald to call Mimi. Funny thing is, it seemed Mimi had been waiting for his call. Donald said she opened up to him about her past and told him everything from all the boys she had in high school to some woman named Sweets who taught her the ropes.

Mimi explained to Donald that she was planning on changing and how she had to because she was pregnant. Loretta thought that Donald took it pretty well. Then again, what could he do or say about the matter. Before hanging up, Mimi asked if it would be possible for her to move in with them for extra support. She made it clear that she could pay her own way and that it was only until she could get on her feet. Going back to school was her main objective; she said needed a GED in order to go to college. Donald informed Mimi he would have to talk to Loretta about it, but once he asked, Loretta was all for it as a firm believer that a person can change any situation through education.

What did shock Loretta about the day was the way Latoya greeted her. She stood in the doorway with Little Man on her hip, smiling as Loretta walked in. That Little Man, all of a two-years-old now, was way too big to be on his momma's hip, was all Loretta could think.

"This is Mimi's step-mother," Latoya said, introducing her to a well-built, nice looking man who stood up and shook Loretta's hand before she could have a seat.

Donald and the children trailed in behind Loretta. The two men shook hands and greeted each other in a manly fashion. Donald Jr. gravitated towards Little Man and Harmony was swept off her feet by Latoya.

"Boy, she looks just like my baby, Mimi, when she was this age. You every bit of my baby girl, all over again," she said looking into Harmony's eyes. Harmony smiled and took in all the warmth Latoya radiated.

Big Momma and Mimi were at the store, getting nutmeg for her sweet potato pies.

"We were just stopping by before we got settled at the hotel," Loretta said.

"Well, have a seat," Latoya said all warm and friendly. "You don't have to leave so soon. The hotel ain't going nowhere."

Before Loretta could take her seat, Latoya said to her, "Would you accompany me in the kitchen to get these gentlemen something to drink?"

"Sure," Loretta said, skeptically. Following Latoya in the kitchen, Loretta was not sure if this was the same woman who she had met awhile back. She looked the same, but her attitude was very different. The room was quiet for a short minute.

Latoya seemed nervous, like she wanted to tell Loretta something, but did not quite know how. The first sign was her opening and closing the refrigerator door. Finally, she sat down at the table and whispered, "Thank you."

Without caring to make her reveal more emotion, Loretta gave her a big hug and whispered in her ear, "You're welcome."

The rest of the evening went well.

Donald and Mimi took to each other well. All the crazed conflicting emotions they dealt with upon their first encounter were erased. She sat in between him and Harmony, looking the perfect picture of what an older daughter should have looked. An innocence that seemed to be new to her person easily replaced the hardened, scared girl who rushed out of the house not so long ago.

Donald's worry of her thinking of him as a stranger was soon replaced with confidence; the same confidence he had when dealing with Harmony. He easily teased Mimi about all the weight she had gained. Mimi laughed at his comments, but Loretta could tell she did not take too kindly to being called fat. What woman would? Weight is never a subject to be toyed with.

Before heading back to the hotel, Mimi and Loretta discussed her baby's father. Mimi shared that he knew of the baby, and that whether or not he would be in the baby's life was totally up to him. Presently, he was married and living in California and the relationship between him and Mimi was just verbal contact. What used to be a real friendship had broken down to him sneaking and calling her every other month to check on her medical condition. Both his wife and mother were upset about the fact that he would even consider the baby being his.

What could Mimi say about that? After all, she was a woman of the night. Without explaining anything to Loretta, Mimi stated he knew he was the father and that was all that mattered.

"It's not important that I be with him," Mimi said, sounding more like she was trying to convince herself. Before turning to leave, she stopped and said, "But it is important that she," Mimi rubbed her stomach, "gets to know him."

41

Willie Joe Johnson

Willie Johnson lay in his uncomfortable sweaty setting, dozing in and out of consciousness and watching. Lately, he found it hard to stay alert. Had it not been for the bugs eating at his lower back area, he would have closed his eyes and drifted on over to wherever the good Lord intended him to be in the first place. What little energy he did have, he used it telling Latoya to get to Mimi. It took all his might to come to Latoya in the form of a dream. True, the family was being pieced back together, but that was not the warning Latoya needed to heed. Trouble was waiting. Did she know there was always calm before the storm?

Willie Johnson fought his slumber. He had been laying there for some time, trying to open his crystal blue eyes. Here lately, his better part was not cooperating with him. He concentrated on the maggots and night bugs eating at the lower area of his body. He could feel as their teeth and claws sunk into his flesh. Even still, the pain barely kept him alert. Finally, in the darkness of his box, Willie Johnson managed to open his eyes wide. With his eyes open, the hot, musty sweat was able to drip into them, burning him to attention. He needed to get to his daughter one last time, needed her to really listen, not just hear what he was saying. Going in a dream form was out of the question, but he knew he would never be able to muster up the energy to go to her physically. Laying in the darkness with his eyes burning like they were two small balls of fire, his mind quickly gave him the answer he needed to get to his daughter. Once he reached her and revealed to her his most urgent message, yet, he cringed hearing his daughter's shrill screams of "Daddy, no!"

42

Mimi Walker

Mimi sat in the living room the evening after the dinner at Big Momma's house feeling content. Over the past few months, she had been speaking to Donald on a regular and he turned out to be wonderful. He was even willing to let her and Imagine, which was the name she had decided to give the baby once she was born, come and live with him. Donald was the only man, besides Tony, that she allowed herself to trust. And trust she did, because for reasons unknown to herself, she opened up and told him everything. Thinking back, maybe it was the emotions that came with having another person growing inside her body. Whatever the reason, it all worked out for the best.

Donald listened like a father was supposed to do. He did not allow judgment to enter their conversation. He gave no excuses or explanations for what had happened in her past. When she was all done with her pity party, he promised he would help her change. After that, the conversations were normal, like him calling to check on her health, asking how her day was going, or her calling so she could speak to her brother and sister.

Mimi went into her bedroom to finish off the book she was reading, *Beloved*. Loretta thought it would be a good idea for Mimi to start sharpening up her reading skills, being that she planned to attend school after having the baby. It had been years since Mimi had touched a book. Serious reading was never a part of her past. Here lately, she had too much free time so reading fit right into her world. Since she found out she was pregnant, she stopped working completely.

Mimi thought the tricks would not be interested in her since her belly was so gigantic, but boy was she wrong about that. She had offers coming out of the woodwork. Men were willing to pay double for what they usually paid a few hundred dollars for. Even though it sounded all good,

Mimi passed them up. She had plenty of money saved, so bills were the least of her problems.

Tony, on the other hand, was a different story. Outside of the once a month call, they had no contact. When he did manage to call, it was short and to the point. He questioned Mimi about her health and asked a few questions about the baby. Only once did he call and the conversation lasted more than forty-five seconds and that particular time, he was drunk. He seemed to be crying about his mother and wife calling him a fool for even considering taking a blood test. How could he possibly believe a whore could be carrying his child?

"I know she's mine," he assured Mimi. "I know you use condoms with your customers. At first, you used them with me." Tony sounded really bad.

Mimi did not know how to respond, so she simply listened. What could she say to make him feel any different? Was he calling so that she could reassure him the baby was his? She knew the blood test would clear up any misunderstandings so comforting Tony was not what she was about to do. Mimi guaranteed Tony that after the test, things would be cleared up.

How she managed to get to that point in her life, she did not understand. Even Sweets' old advice would not be able to clear any of Mimi's new problems. Sweets never had a child. Her only love was Dollar Bill. How would she be able to compare his love to that of a child? All the crazy thoughts Mimi was going through danced in her head making her look at a different life; a life she wanted no part of, but was now forced to figure out how to maneuver through.

Raising a child? Mimi never envisioned herself as a momma. She wondered would she be the momma she wanted or would she be the mother she received? Before all the changes entered her life, Mimi knew it all. Mimi knew she would never be like Latoya. Growing up, she knew if she had a daughter of her own, she would be the perfect mother.

That day, her mindset was different. In the past, Tony did not matter, when he walked away from the restaurant it hurt, but she was prepared to accept that he was no longer part of her life. Today, he was important.

Her baby girl would need him. Mimi liked to try and convince herself that her feelings for him were due to the baby but, deep in her heart, she knew she wanted Tony as much as her child would need him. How Mimi went from wanting Tony to needing him was something she could not quite figure out. She decided to continue reading the book because all these new questions she did not have the energy or the know-how to try and answer.

"So a whore actually uses a bed for sleeping?" a voice said.

Mimi looked up and saw Mrs. Knott, Tony's mother, standing in her bedroom and wondered if she had left her apartment door unlocked again.

Mrs. Knott's stood in her doorway looking all of a deacon's wife. She wore a pair of tree bark-colored pants and a tea-colored turtleneck. She had on low-heeled black shoes with a brown bow attached to the sides and she sported her hair in a French roll, with a side bang.

Her eyes, on the other hand, revealed something totally different from her external appearance. They seemed to be heavy with both anger and grief. She panted like a mad woman and slowly inched her way toward Mimi, exposing the fact that she had a gun in her right hand.

"What are you doing in my apartment?" Mimi managed to say, after realizing she was not dreaming.

"I can pick a lock better than you can suck a dick," the woman spat at her. A slick grin spread across Mrs. Knott's face. She seemed to be taking pleasure in the fact that she was able to degrade Mimi. She walked closer to Mimi's bed and sat down. "I never could stand your kind, you whore."

Mrs. Knott looked at the wall as she spoke.

"I have had to deal with the likes of you my entire life. First, there was your mother. Yea, she had a fling with my husband in her younger days. What did I do? I did the right thing; I called your grandmother up and allowed her to straighten it out. Oh, believe me when I tell you I wanted to act a monkey—cut up all his clothes, burn down the house, put sugar in his tank, pack up my child and leave, and all the other stuff us *mad* black women do when we pissed."

Mrs. Knott turned and looked Mimi in the eye, and her voice softened.

"I wasn't allowed to do that, being that I'm a deacon's wife. Lord forbid anyone in the congregation find out Deacon Knott is sleeping with Big Momma's illegitimate daughter. What would become of the church? What would become of the poor people's souls who waited patiently every Sunday for that God-fearing man to help conduct the happenings of the church; those all-important deeds that my good-for-nothing husband was put on Earth to help conduct. No, I couldn't expose him in such a manner, and besides, I was a compliant wife."

Mrs. Knott's eyes teared up and her voice cracked as she continued, "I actually thought that if I did right by my man, stand by his side, forgive him and take him back, things would get better from there.

"Things did get better for a while. I had to have been a fool to think things would stay that way, though. Him coming home every night, us doing special things together, true relationship stuff—that good stuff. It got to the point that I all but put Latoya out of my mind. I started believing what everybody else at church was believing: that my husband was a true man of God, that my husband loved me and had only made a mistake. Started thinking it was a good thing that I didn't walk out on him.

"I guess I got beside myself, becoming proud of him, 'cause when I wasn't looking, and when I got comfortable and started trusting him again, was when I found out about Sweets. Thinking back, I must have let it go on too long, because when I confronted him, he simply looked at me. That joker didn't say a word. Just looked me in the eyes as if to say, 'Well, now you know.'"

Mimi shifted her heavy belly, trying to find a comfortable spot in all the confusion that had just positioned itself on her bed.

This woman is mad,' Mimi thought. If Sweets was seeing Mr. Knott, Mimi felt she would have known. Listening to the crazy woman ramble, Mimi decided to inch herself closer to the side of the bed that was closest to bedroom door — not that she could run fast with all the extra weight the baby had put on her but, she felt, if she needed to make a run for it, being close to the door would only help her situation.

"Where you think you going?" Mrs. Knott's screamed and slapped Mimi across the face with the pistol, knocking her on the floor and leaving a bloody gash on the side of her face.

"I intend to do to you what I did to that slut-ass friend of yours, Sweets. You won't make it out of this room alive."

Mimi gasped realizing she was looking at Sweets' killer. Mrs. Knott stood over Mimi with rage clouding her eyes.

"All of you make my skin crawl. First, your momma tried to ruin my marriage. Later, that nasty-ass friend of yours came waltzing into my marriage. Here it is, years later, and you trying to plant some bastard child on my son? I thought Sweets was the last whore I'd have to send to her grave. Guess the Lord had more work for me to do."

Mimi lay on the floor, only half conscious. Warm salty blood dripped directly from her wound into her mouth. Her head pounded sending throbbing pain throughout her entire body. Mimi slowly wrapped her arms around her stomach. Lying on the floor, she recalled a newspaper article about a mother being shot but the baby living through the terrible ordeal. The baby had some complications, but doctors managed to deliver the baby safely.

It was a girl.

At that very moment, Mimi knew she wanted her child, Imagine, to live. She closed her eyes and said a prayer, an unselfish prayer, that consisted of asking the Lord to please let her baby live— the same child Mimi had not long ago asked Him to take away. Mimi pleaded with Him to save her baby. She had no doubt that the Lord would answer her prayer and felt that, this particular time, all would go as she planned. After saying the prayer, Mimi closed her eyes and prepared herself for death.

"No!" Latoya yelled as she rushed through the bedroom door. She dove toward Mrs. Knott, knocking the gun from her hand. The gun went off, breaking a window as it slid across the floor, landing by Mimi's leg.

The sound of gunfire forced Mimi to open her eyes. Mimi lay there gazing at the weapon. She had no strength; she was completely drained of all energy. The taste of the warm blood had begun to settle in her throat. Not only was her head pounding, but her body was aching. Mimi watched as both women struggled on the floor. Mrs. Knott had somehow managed to pin Latoya down and was banging her head on the floor.

Mimi watched helplessly as her mother was being beaten by the crazed old woman.

'I gotta do something,' Mimi thought. She tried pushing herself up by her arms, but quickly became light-headed and lay back down. Mimi stared at the gun, wishing it would get up and come to her. Peering over at the two women struggling, she saw that Latoya had managed to get her arms around Mrs. Knott's neck and was choking her.

Mimi said one more prayer— this time asking the Lord to give her the strength to do whatever He felt was right that she should do. With that, Mimi managed to kick the gun toward her hand and pick it up. By then, Latoya had gotten out of Mrs. Knott's grip. She ran and grabbed the gun from Mimi's hand, and within minutes, it was all over.

Mrs. Knott lay in a puddle of her own blood in the middle of Mimi's bedroom floor. Latoya dropped the gun on the bed and, with tears in her eyes, helped Mimi to the bed.

"Thank you, Daddy," Latoya said as she dialed 911.

www.ingramcontent.com/pod-product-compliance
Lightning Source LLC
Chambersburg PA
CBHW050524260626
47157CB00004B/1452